Alex A. Zudor

Vox Populi

An Agent Strabo Mystery (#1)

ISBN: 9798396357112

Cover design by: Ingrid Zudor
Published in the United States of America

IN MEMORY OF MY GRANDMOTHER,

Lucretia Bulz

1932 – 2001

For she sparked my love for all things historical

Table of Contents

Foreword to the Revised Edition

As a child, my favorite time of the day was the evening electricity blackout. Naturally, you might ask yourself what a scheduled blackout is and why on Earth I enjoyed them.

In the '80s, my country of birth was among the harshest communist dictatorships in Europe. Unlike other countries in the Eastern Block, many basic things were rationalized due to an imbecilic economic policy, electricity among them. But when the lights went out, the magic started.

My father regaled me with stories from the past, and vivid images of heroic warriors and beautiful princesses filled the dark rooms of our cramped flat. None I loved more than those about the Ancient Romans.

The years went by, and I grew up, dedicating most of my adult life to a corporate career in the hyper-capitalistic environment of recent decades. Ironically, it took another wave of enforced restrictions to remind me of the fascinating stories of my childhood.

We were living in Hong Kong when the covid-19 epidemic began, so we found ourselves holed up in a tiny apartment as the lockdowns came into force. Bored out of my skull and ignored most of the time by my equally exasperated wife, I found refuge in Ancient Rome—it is how I wrote the present book, my first *Agent Strabo Roman Mystery* novella. Since then, I have renounced my corporate executive job, focusing on the things I love—writing historical fiction is one of them.

The story is set 250 years after Gaius Iulius Caesar was stabbed to death on the Senate floor. The first African Emperor had just ascended to the Purple, heralding a gradual power shift from the old Italian aristocracy to the self-made military *equites* of the provinces. To reflect the emerging trend, our hero is a legionary veteran from the province of

Dacia (or *Tres Daciae*), in what is today my birth country of Romania.

Lucius Lucretius Strabo will soon become a *frumentarius*, a member of the Roman Empire's special service. Initially responsible for the legions' grain supply, the *Frumentarii* morphed into the Empire's secret policemen, spy agents, military couriers, and covert operatives. Although *frumentum* means grain, don't let the innocuous name fool you—their reputation was so ferocious that Emperor Diocletian had to disband them in the early 4th Century AD.

I have to warn you; the book contains a few Latin words. I believe it adds a bit of flavor, so I hope you won't mind—their meaning should become evident once you read on.

While on the topic of Latin, I took the liberty to forego the vocative case when referring to names. For example, instead of *Porcie,* I kept the nominative form, Porcius. Some Latin-speaking readers might find this objectionable; however, the book being in English, I believe Latin grammar doesn't apply in this case. By the way, my Latin is rudimentary, at best, so I apologize for any other grammar mistakes.

Lastly, please note that *Agent Strabo's Roman Mysteries* are novella-length, circa 20.000 words each (around 100 A4 pages). I believe it balances my desire for a fast-paced narrative and the length needed for proper character building. My aim was to create the literary equivalent of today's crime & action TV series.

Without further ado, let Strabo's first mystery begin.

Regards,

Alex A. Zudor

March 2023

I. Fortune Favors the Drunk

Strabo slowly opened his remaining eye. His head throbbed as he struggled to adjust to the dim light.

He was in his room, lying on the uncomfortable straw pallet serving as his bed. He ran a cursory inspection of himself. All his body parts were in order. *Almost all*, he reminded himself bitterly.

It seemed he had passed out the previous night wearing his legionary sandals and the once-red tunic that came with the job. At least he was already dressed up.

Strabo turned his head sideways to take in the rest of the scene.

He counted three empty wine flagons lined up on the floor next to his pallet. The whole room reeked, and the sour vinegary smell of cheap wine filled the air. In the opposite corner, several cockroaches feasted on a discarded Lucanian sausage and a piece of soggy bread.

After an epic internal struggle, Strabo decided to get on his feet.

Fuck, my head explodes!

He walked dizzily to the sole window of his fourth-floor room. The midday summer sun was shining down on the city. The streets below the apartment building were crowded at this time of day.

I need to pee.

Strabo considered relieving himself in the corner for a fleeting moment but then decided against it. He didn't want to disturb his roommates, the cockroaches.

He kneeled next to the pallet, lifted one of the loose floorboards, and grabbed a handful of coins from his dwindling stash. When he was discharged on medical grounds almost five months ago, Strabo received a reward of 1500 *denarii* and a small plot of land several miles north of the city. It should be enough to drink himself to an early grave, and he also had the land on which to dig it.

Strabo left his room and stepped into the dark staircase. He cursed. *That bitch Aquilina is saving on the lamp oil again.*

As he stumbled down the stairs, the typical aroma of a Roman tenement hit him. The smell of cooking, the acrid odor of old sweat, and the reek of shit and piss blended into the unmistakable scent of an *insula.*

Strabo's descent offered a cursory but reasonably accurate glimpse into the Roman social hierarchy. The lower one lived, the higher one was on the pecking order.

Unlike the pitch-black fourth floor, the third was lit by a single oil lamp, while on the second, one lamp burned next to the doors of each of the three large apartments. Still, the first floor was the Temple of Sol by comparison—four large oil lamps illuminated the access to a couple of luxury apartments.

Parasites live in luxury, while heroes struggle in squalid little shitholes.

"Welcome to the fucking Roman Empire!" Strabo shouted into the empty staircase.

One of the doors led to Aquilina's suite, his landlady and owner of the building. Strabo considered peeing on it but then again, maybe not. Aquilina was a colossal woman gifted with broad shoulders, fists of stone, and a well-documented penchant for using her abilities to sort out troublemaking tenants.

Once on the ground floor, Strabo walked by the *ianitor* and out the gate—the porter was unwilling to interrupt his sullen contemplation of the dusty floor by acknowledging the ill-reputed tenant.

Strabo shielded his face from the sudden shock of bright sunlight, but there was nothing he could do about the head-splitting noise. The northern side of the tenement fronted the *decumanus maximus*, the city's east-west avenue, so his auditory senses were flooded by chit-chatting neighbors, shouting vendors, whinnying horses, playing children, and gurgling water.

I need to pee, the inner voice nagged him.

The ground floor hosted a *fullonica*, a public laundry. As customary, several recipients were placed in front of it, encouraging the inhabitants to discard their piss-pots there—urine was the primary stain-removing substance in the fuller's washing tubs.

Strabo lifted his tunic, finally relieving himself—decorum was a luxury he couldn't afford. After giving it a final squeeze and a few shakes, he let his tunic down and turned towards his favorite wine shop when.....WHAM! He violently ran into a passerby.

"*Stultissime!*" came the victim's sharp retort. "Watch where you're going, you bloody idiot!"

Strabo swallowed a stream of invectives, for he recognized the unforgettable voice. The man was Gnaeus Manlius Hilarius, his former commander.

"Do I know you?" Hilarius said suspiciously. "You look fam…Good Gods! It is none other than Legionary Strabo." He looked over his former subordinate, disgust replacing anger as he noted Strabo's appearance. "What in the name of Jupiter happened to you?"

"Nothing, *Prime Pile*, sir! Everything is fine and dandy," Strabo barked, standing at attention.

Hilarius wrinkled his nose. "You reek. When was the last time you visited the baths?"

"A true hero doesn't need baths, sir! Nor respect or consideration! We only need to serve the Empire until discarded like garbage."

The distinguished officer seemed to find Strabo's comments somewhat disagreeable. Hilarius turned red from his bull-like neck to the top of his bald head, an angry growl rising from his throat.

"Legionary Strabo, pull yourself together!" he eventually erupted.

Passers-by turned their heads, curious to see what all the commotion was about.

Hilarius took a calming breath and added, "Look here, Strabo, you received your *praemia* and got a piece of land. You have more than most."

"What about the respect of my fellow citizens?" Strabo asked. "I am just another cripple, a good-for-nothing half-man as far as everybody is concerned." He tried to keep his angry tears from swelling. "Street urchins call me the Cyclops, and women turn their heads away when they pass by me. "How about that, sir?"

Hilarius shook his head repeatedly, struggling to find the words to express his disappointment. He eventually straightened up, crossed his arms on his chest, and addressed Strabo, scorn permeating every word. "Disgraceful! And to think you were a legionary just a few months ago." The officer pushed on. "You know why women turn their heads when you pass by them?" He poked Strabo's chest with his finger. "Because," poke, "you," poke, "stink!" poke.

Strabo was dumbstruck. Before he could gather his wits, however, Hilarius continued his tirade.

"You still have both hands, both legs, your brain, and one working eye. Most importantly, you still have your fucking life as opposed to the hundreds of our comrades who died at Lugdunum."

Shame, anger, and a host of other contradictory feelings washed over Strabo's entire being.

"If you decide to man up and stop this nonsense, drop by the *Procurator*'s Office. I will be there until after the elections." With that said, Hilarius turned and strode away, leaving Strabo in an even more confused state than he was in before.

******

An hour later, Strabo nurtured a flagon of cheap wine in front of his favorite tavern named *Cuculus*, the Cuckoo. The so-called wine shop was a glorified hole-in-the-wall, the product on offer as dubious as the establishment itself. Judging by the taste—and the resulting hangover he was so familiar with—Strabo suspected the wine wasn't even the ordinary *posca* but plain vinegar mixed with water.

Strabo sat on the sidewalk, watching the people passing by, all of them busy going about their lives. *At least they have a life.*

He had difficulties recalling the days when he had reasons to wake up in the mornings and the drive to keep on going despite the obstacles Fortuna threw at him. However, it wasn't so long ago.

It is that bloody Hilarius! Don't let him get to you.

Drinking like there was no tomorrow worked out just fine, he tried to reassure himself. But the words rang hollow for the first time in months.

He was born Lucius Lucretius Strabo in the provincial metropolis of Ulpia Traiana Sarmizegetusa during the 14th regnal year of Caesar Marcus Aurelius Antoninus Augustus. It was a pompous way of saying that he was 22 years old and was from around town.

He hated both farming and violence, but since he was terrible at the former and reasonably competent at the latter, he joined the legions six years ago, lying about his age so he could enlist before his eighteenth birthday.

Alas, Marcus Aurelius' son and successor, Emperor Commodus, insisted on pissing everybody off with his megalomania and crazy gladiatorial shit, among other things. Eventually, he got himself assassinated a few months after Strabo joined the Eagles.

Vale Pax Romana, Salve Chaos! Goodbye Roman Peace, Hello Chaos!

The ensuing civil war shattered a century of internal stability and prosperity.

Now that's what I call perfect timing.

During the next five years, Strabo got to see the world as part of Septimius Severus' empire-wide tour of death and destruction.

At long last, since Fortuna was a generous little goddess, she decided Strabo shouldn't go home empty-handed but rather empty-socketed. In the final battle of the Roman-on-Roman power struggle, a howling legionary from Britannia poked out Strabo's left eye using his standard issue *gladius* just as he was regularly stabbed in the belly by a diligent Legionary Strabo.

After the unfortunate incident, Strabo learned that *Legio XIII Gemina*'s taste for twins goes beyond its name. It actually expects its members to have a pair of everything: two hands, two legs, and two eyes, so Strabo was discharged on medical grounds.

In recognition of his service and the crippling wounds he received in combat, Strabo was awarded a *missio causaria,* including several years' worth of salary and a deed to a plot in the middle of nowhere. As a bonus, he was officially inducted into the *honestiores* class of distinguished citizens.

I was back to square one.

With the army no longer an option, returning to his father's rural estate was again on the table. However, moving back with his parents wasn't his idea of moving ahead in life, and farming his own land sounded even less appealing.

To add to his woes, he couldn't get used to being a cripple— Strabo hadn't realized before how attached he was to his body parts. So he drank. And drank. And drank some more while planning to keep doing so until the end of his days.

That fucking Hilarius had to ruin it all!

Strabo never liked the man, to be honest. From the first time they met, he found the esteemed *Primus Pilus* a humorless jerk. It was hilarious that he was called Hilarius. However,

Strabo had to admit he was a decent commander who cared for his men.

Hilarius was a batshit crazy, ice-cold, stick-in-the-ass officer who rose to one of the highest rank an enlisted man could dream of by leading from the front and climbing on the corpses of the enemy warriors he personally dispatched. His kill count was probably comparable to the average population of a decent provincial town, if not higher. Also, the Senior Centurion made sure his men had everything they needed to be an effective killing machine: lots of drilling and marching, spotless equipment, good food, enough wine, and even the occasional woman when the circumstances allowed it. Lastly, he avoided wasting lives on stupid or ill-conceived missions. It was why he put such a high price on military intelligence—a fascinating concept if one could look beyond the contradiction in terms.

Whenever a new military campaign began, Hilarius appointed a few men to act as intelligence gatherers. For some reason or another, Strabo was one of the select few. Perhaps it was because of his extraordinary powers of observation or his superior intelligence, military or otherwise. Nonetheless, Strabo proved to be a gifted spy. Sometimes he was sent ahead of the army to collect information in taverns and brothels or to track enemy movements. Other times, Strabo investigated suspicious activities within the legion, exposing enemy spies or assassin wannabes.

It was an exciting existence, and it kept Strabo away from the dull routine of army life and most of the mindless killing associated with war. Now that he thought about it, working as an intelligence agent was the closest he had ever gotten to his theoretical dream job. It didn't involve farming, it required only a minimal amount of killing, and it came with all the other benefits of an army job—secure pay, medical benefits, retirement fund, and a respectable position in society.

He sighed. "I guess I have good old Hilarius to thank for that," Strabo said out loud.

"What's so hilarious? Do you want a piece of me?" one of the other customers said.

"Calm down, Porcius. I was talking to myself. Nothing is hilarious except...," Strabo paused. "It just struck me how appropriate your name is. Looking at you, I can't stop thinking of pigs, you know?"

"Look who's talking! Squinty Stinky!

The word *strabo* literally meant cross-eyed or squinty. For some reason or another, he had carried the nickname since early childhood, but now that he had lost one eye, it suited him even better. However, he had strong objections to being called Stinky—he had lived in filth only for the last few months.

At least somebody was in a good mood.

Porcius' manic laughter turned into a wet, choking cough. Strabo worried his comrade would die right then and there, and he would be accused of killing him—murder by hilarity. *That's hilarious.* He smiled. *Not fucking Hilarius again. I almost forgot about him.*

"Porcius, what's the news in town?" Strabo said, trying to distract himself from the upcoming epiphany.

"Nothing. Even the electoral campaign stinks, Stinky." Porcius grinned. "While Poplicola and his sidekick, Mus, are putting up a good fight for the upcoming *aediles* election, they have no chance of winning."

"Why?" Strabo said. "I thought Poplicola was all the rage and the Everyman *humiliores*, and even the distinguished *honestiores* were passionately in love with him."

"Old news, Stinky. Where do you live, man? In a cave?" Porcius bellowed, obviously delighted by his buddy's ignorance.

"If Aquilina had heard what you just said, she would skin you alive," Strabo said, taking his index finger to his mouth in a silencing gesture.

"Never mind the bitch. I'm not even sure she is a woman, mind you. Some say she is a former male wrestler with a penchant for cross-dressing."

Strabo laughed. "What are you talking about? I think the *posca* had eaten away what was left of your brain."

Porcius looked hurt. "Just be careful not to bend down when *she* is around. You know what I mean?" He leered, the gaps in his dental equipment revealing themselves in all their terrible splendor.

"Anyway, back to our topic, Septimius Geta, our beloved Governor, announced his support for Varro and Lentulus. Do you think our city fathers and the other *honestiores* will vote against the wishes of the Emperor's brother?" Porcius paused for rhetorical effect before he answered his own question, "No, *amice*." He shook his head. "They will not only vote for Varro and Lentulus on election day, but they will go head over heels to show their public support during the rest of the campaign."

Strabo bristled, fake outrage on his face. "Porcius, are you implying our electoral system is rigged? That is treason, I say!" Strabo thundered, his right hand's index finger pointing toward the sky. "It is our sacred duty, as citizens of this great Empire of ours, to vote for whoever our Emperor tells us to."

"Fuck off, Stinky." Porcius waved dismissively.

"Well, *frater*, that's what I'll do without hesitation." Strabo decided to embrace the only honorable course of action now that Hilarius had given him a piece of his mind. "I have an appointment at the *Procurator*'s Office."

"The *Procurator*'s Office, he says." Porcius' derisive words were addressed to Strabo's departing figure.

II. The Making of a *Frumentarius*

The clean waters of the *Nymphaeum*, the monumental fountain near the city center, acted as a perfect mirror in the early morning light. Strabo stared into the water, and a proper Roman citizen looked back at him.

He contemplated the extraordinary effects of a brief and unpleasant exchange. One moment he was in the bottomless pit of despair, and the next, he cleaned his room, laundered his soiled legionary tunic, and shopped for new clothing and furniture. Then he visited the baths at the New Forum and scrubbed himself clean—no more Squinty Stinky.

It felt like suddenly waking up from a long, long nightmare.

Maybe Strabo had hit rock bottom, and all he needed was somebody to grab him by the hair and lift him from the deep pool of despair. Or perhaps time slowly healed his troubled soul, and meeting Hilarius at the right moment was just a lucky coincidence. Whatever it was, Strabo felt like a different man this morning, determined to attach some degree of meaning to his life.

He hoped beyond hope that Hilarius would have a job or errand for him. But no matter how desperate his situation was, he still wouldn't consider farming. In the worst-case scenario, he'll go back to drinking with Porcius and eating with the cockroaches.

Earlier, after the first wine-free night in a long while, he called on the *tonsor* based on Aquilina's tenement's ground floor. He got a proper haircut, a thorough shave, and the best facial treatment available. Then he put on his new white tunic and the exquisite leather belt with the bronze buckle he had acquired yesterday. The cherry on the top was his new calfskin eyepatch—its color matched the nuance of the belt, the buckle, and the old sandals.

Ecce homo! A fashion icon was born.

Satisfied with his appearance, he proceeded toward the *Procurator*'s Office.

The *locus groma*, the place where the city's two main avenues intersected, was just a few dozen steps away from the fountain. Strabo turned northwards on the *cardo maximus*, the main north-south avenue, approaching the large building complex serving as the *Procurator*'s Office.

The *Procurator* of Dacia Apulensis was the most senior official based in the city of Sarmizegetusa. He was in charge of the provincial administration's financial affairs and acted as *de facto* deputy governor. The complex reflected its prominent resident's status, currently a certain Lucius Petronius Antonius. It served not only as Antonius' residence but also hosted some of the countless administrators needed to run the province.

Strabo stopped in front of the southern wing's entrance. A couple of legionaries stood guard in full gear, and everything about their looks screamed, "Hilarius is our boss!" They were well-fed, but the lack of fat indicated constant drilling. Their purely utilitarian equipment was in perfect condition, and, most tellingly, they were the embodiment of the articles of military regulations describing guard duty—straight back, legs close together, eyes front, the spear in the right hand pointing to the sky, and the shield held upright with the left hand.

Who could stand motionlessly in the heat of a summer morning, dressed in heavy armor, while staring straight into the sun? Without fidgeting or showing any sign of discomfort?

Only a *tyrannus superbus* like Hilarius could instill fear to the necessary degree to maintain such discipline.

"Mornin', boys, is the boss in?"

"Piss off," one of the brutalized legionaries said. The fact that he replied without moving a single muscle, not even the ocular ones, was telling.

"I am Lucius Lucretius Strabo here to see *Primus Pilus* Gnaeus Manlius Hilarius," Strabo said. "He is expecting me."

"*Primus pilus*?" The guard sneered.

"We have no senior centurions around. Try the fortress at Apulum," his twin brother said.

Strabo had a moment of doubt. *Could I be wrong? Have I lost my deductive powers?*

"Come on, guys. Don't fuck with me," Strabo said. "I met Hilarius yesterday on the *decumanus*. He told me to drop by if I need a job." He pointed to his missing eye. "See the patch? I got it earlier touring with the First *Cohors* of the *Gemina*. Lugdunum, nice place; you might have heard of it."

The guards looked at each other.

"Eh." Brother number one grunted.

"Uh," the twin echoed. Such a severe breach of guarding protocols could get them to latrine duty for a week.

Finally, brother number one turned to Strabo. "You choose a bad day to call in, *frater*. All hell broke loose during the night, and Hilarius is in a foul mood." The twin continued, "If you served under him, you know what it means, right?"

"Avoid getting into visual range at any cost, but if you are unfortunate enough to get into range, back off slowly and hope he hasn't noticed you already."

The twins nodded appreciatively at Strabo's wise words.

They suddenly straightened, eyes front and all, because they heard footsteps from inside.

Two men walked out of the building, clearly agitated and unhappy. They passed between the guards and by Strabo without a glance and walked hurriedly towards the Old Forum. Strabo recognized the two sitting *duumviri*, Verres and Aculeo.

"Our two distinguished mayors look distinctly unhealthy today," Strabo said. "Food poisoning, perhaps?" He thought he was funny, but the twins winced simultaneously at his remarks.

More footsteps echoed from inside, this time the heavy stomp of hobnailed boots. A couple of heartbeats later, the man himself stormed out of the building. Hilarius glanced at them as he passed, stopped as if forgetting something, then turned toward the twins, murder in his eyes.

"You think you are on some fucking city tour, chatting up the locals when on guard duty?" His nostrils flared. "And you, citizen, go about your business, no lollygagging."

"*Prime Pile*, sir, it is me, Legionary Strabo. You told me to call on you if I—" he paused momentarily. "If I change my mind."

Hilarius squinted as if to see him better. "Ah, I barely recognized you without your distinctive aroma." He smiled weakly at his own joke. "Look, son, you chose the worst possible moment. Look me up after the election."

Strabo considered the situation for a heartbeat and took a deep breath. "I can help with the poisoning," he blurted.

If looks could kill, the twins would have dropped to the floor instantly. "What did these idiots tell you?" Hilarius' voice was low and menacing.

"Nothing, sir. That is, they didn't tell me anything important by using words."

Hilarius rolled his eyes knowingly. "Here we go again."

"I came to call on you, sir, as you kindly suggested the other day. The twins opined I should skip today's visit due to some unfortunate developments over the night. Then, I saw the *duumviri* hurrying out as if looking for the latrine after a meal of bad oysters. I jokingly observed as much, but the two gents winced instead of smiling. Just now, you asked me to call on you after the elections, confirming your foul mood, sir." Strabo paused for breath. He knew his following words might be decisive. "Adding all these up, I concluded that somebody was poisoned, that it is somehow related to the upcoming elections, and that the circumstances are worrying enough to ruin the day of our city's leaders and the First Spear of the Thirteenth." He stroked his chin. "This last part doesn't make sense, though. Why are you involved, sir? Was the victim a military man?"

Hilarius chortled. Actually, it was more akin to a bark. Strabo could not be certain.

"If you hadn't spent the previous months in Bacchus' firm embrace, you would have known by now that I was promoted to Camp Praefect of the Thirteenth Legion."

"Congratulations, sir," Strabo said in an even voice.

"Fuck off, Strabo. I am a soldier, not a glorified *maior domus*." Even the terrified guards smiled at the last comment. Hilarius ignored them and added, "I was temporarily deputized to the *Procurator*'s Office to ensure an incident-free election campaign."

"My sincere condolences, sir. The victim's untimely death must have hit you hard, whoever he was."

"You crack me up, Strabo." Hilarius glanced at the guards. "Isn't he the funniest dead man walking you've ever seen?"

"I am sorry, *Praefecte*. I just thought to lighten the mood."

"Unfortunately, the rest of your deductions were not far from the truth." The Praefect shook his head as if pondering a difficult decision. "You were always too smart for your own good, Strabo. But, once again, your skills might be useful to the Empire."

******

Somebody was poisoned, all right. The victim was one of the gentlemen running for next year's *aedile*-ship: Cominius Pontius Poplicola.

"What do we know about the circumstances, sir?" Strabo said. They were inside Hilarius' temporary office, the commander sitting behind his desk, Strabo on a stool opposite.

"According to his wife, Aurelia Sexta, he got sick at home after attending a dinner party. He left the marital bed during the night, complaining about tingling in the throat. His wife found him in the morning. He died on the *latrina*." Hilarius shook his head. "A shitty way to go."

Bitter rivalries during elections were not uncommon, but the days of political violence were long gone. Actually, political violence was never a thing in the colonies since the prize was seldom worth killing or dying for.

The big decisions were made in Rome or the Governor's Palace at Apulum, not the local *curia*. Still, wealthy young men who dreamed of a successful career beyond Sarmisegetuza's walls had to acquire a degree of administrative experience before being eligible to command one of the auxiliary cohorts. The alternative route was to serve as a priest for a couple of years before joining the army.

"Are we certain it was deliberate poisoning?" Strabo said. "He could have eaten something bad at home or a *taberna*."

"Aurelia Sexta was adamant her late husband went straight to bed after returning home. And his running mate, Furius Mus, claims to have been at his side all day long. No food or drink from public establishments was consumed."

Strabo stroked his chin in contemplation. "They might be mistaken or might be lying. Could any of them have poisoned him?"

"I am told Aurelia and Poplicola were one of those strange couples who married for love." The Praefect made such a sour face that Strabo worried he would vomit on the elegant marble floor. "Love," Hilarius repeated the seemingly alien concept. "What the fuck has love got to do with marriage?"

"Indeed, *Praefecte*, why would anyone choose to live with someone they actually feel attracted to?"

As often happened, sarcasm bounced off Hilarius. He nodded, agreeing with Strabo's comment.

Mrs. Manlius must be a delightful woman to elicit this level of devotion.

"What about his running mate? Angry-us or something, I forgot his name."

"You never met Gaius Furius Mus, I reckon. Well, how could I best describe him?" The Praefect paused. "Let me put it like this; Mus is unelectable. Even his loving mother wouldn't vote for him if we were crazy enough to let women vote. So his only hope to become a magistrate was as Poplicola's insignificant other." Hilarius shook his head. "When Poplicola croaked, Mus lost his ticket to relevance. He had everything to lose and nothing to gain from his mate's death."

Strabo nodded, tending to acquiesce to Hilarius' conclusion, although he wasn't entirely convinced. But, since the Praefect was unmistakably proud of his deduction, Strabo decided against ruining one of Hilarius' rare moments of intellectual fulfillment. So he swallowed a smart-ass remark and said instead, "Let's discuss the dinner party, sir. Perhaps the host had a terrible cook. You know, one of those cooking-is-an-art types."

"Unlikely. Unfortunately, no other guest is sick or dead," the officer said bitterly.

Strabo couldn't hide his astonishment. "Gnaeus Manlius, are you developing a sense of humor by any chance?"

"First of all, I am *Praefectus* Hilarius to you, ex-Legionary Strabo. Second, what the hell are you talking about, sonny?"

"Apologies, sir, but let me get this straight. Do you actually wish somebody else would have died?"

"But of course! It would have made things so much easier." Hilarius sighed, then explained, "If other guests had died, it would mean Poplicola was not deliberately poisoned."

"Right, sir. The more, the merrier, as I always say."

"Yes, especially with that useless lot. We would be better off if they would just, you know...." He moved his thumb horizontally over his throat. "Go away."

"Yes, sir, of course. You are right, as always. Could you be a bit more specific, though? Who exactly are we talking about?"

"The dinner party, man, the bloody dinner. Focus!" Hilarius snapped. "It was organized by one of the *duumviri*, the fat one, Verres, at his city house. The entire gang attended: the co-*duumvir* Aculeo, the current pair of *aediles* Macula and Merula, the Poplicola-Mus duo, and their counter candidates, Varro and Lentulus." A dreamy smile crossed Hilarius' face as he gazed into the middle distance. "Just imagine them writhing on the floor, foaming mouths and gasping for air... Ah, things would be much simpler without these political animals."

Creepy. Strabo shuddered. Then he said, "One can always dream, sir. But, getting back to the topic at hand, that is quite an eminent list of suspects. Do you have anybody else in mind?"

"As a matter of fact, I do have somebody else in mind," Hilarius said, trying to find a diplomatic way of expressing his suspicions. "Our governor, Publius Septimius Geta, publicly endorsed the Varro-Lentulus ticket against the Poplicola-Mus pair. Under normal circumstances, nobody would give a wet shit about the Governor's endorsement. Legates come and go, and the current one has already been here for almost three years—he'll leave soon."

Strabo scratched his head. "I heard something about it from my buddy Porcius."

"However, our incumbent Legate is not your usual garden variety governor, as you well know. He is the Emperor's baby brother! So all the local leaders and leader wannabes are falling head over heels to kiss ass and support Geta's pet candidates." The Praefect paused, giving Strabo a bit of time to digest the situation. Then he continued, "The question is the following, does getting on the Imperial Baby Brother's good side worth killing for? And the answer seems to be in the affirmative."

Hilarius sighed heavily. Strabo got a glimpse beyond his former commander's killing-machine persona for the first time since they had known each other.

"Honestly, I couldn't care less," Hilarius said eventually. "Politicians are like rats or cockroaches. One can never exterminate them all. I would have enjoyed killing the oily bastard Poplicola myself—bare hands on his neck, eyes bulging as he slowly turns blue...."

"So why the long face, sir?"

The Praefect ignored him. "However, the civil war ended only a few short months ago. Severus' claim to the Imperial Purple is strenuous at best. Many of the Emperor's enemies are still in the Senate or scattered across the provinces and the legions, waiting for an opportunity to strike back."

"I see."

"Since Severus is away from Rome, looking for a rematch with our old friends, the Parthians, it could be the right moment to stir trouble at home. All one needs to do is to fan the flames of discontent."

"I begin to see the problem, sir," Strabo said.

"No matter how preposterous the allegations might sound, it wouldn't take a Cicero to convince our colony's inhabitants that their favorite political star was poisoned at the Governor's orders. And if Geta was involved, the Emperor was involved." Hilarius shuddered. "The news would travel faster than lightning throughout the Empire—bad news and celebrity scandals always do. The story would take epic proportions by the time it reached Rome, Germania, and Hispania. Poplicola would be painted as a revenant Sempronius Gracchus, silenced because he championed the People against Severus' tyranny."

Before asking the obvious, Strabo considered the situation for a long while. "Why are you telling me all this, *Praefecte?*"

"You were one of my best intelligence agents during the civil war. Although you can't be a legionary anymore due to your…mmm…sacrifice, you could be attached to the Thirteenth Legion as a *frumentarius.*"

"Me, sir? A special agent?"

"Was your hearing damaged as well? Yes, a bloody *frumentarius*! An agent of the Imperial not-so-secret service."

"No, sir. I mean, yes, sir. You know what I mean!" Strabo struggled to articulate his thoughts. "To your question, my hearing is fine, and it would be an honor to serve the Empire once more. And you, of course, to serve under your—"

"Cut the bullshit!" Hilarius snapped. "I got it; you are delighted to take the job. You might live to regret it sooner rather than later, though." He left the sentence hanging. "Now, the rules are simple." The Praefect counted on his fingers. "First rule: you report to me and only to me. Second rule: no more sissy fits or stinkiness. Third rule: you never fail me. NEVER. EVER!" He held Strabo's gaze for several heartbeats to drive the point through. "Am I clear?"

"Crystal, sir, even clearer than crystal, clearer than ten crystals combined, as clear as the waters of—" Strabo nodded earnestly.

"I'll take that as a *yes.*"

Hilarius rose solemnly, Strabo with him, and declared in a ceremonious voice, "I, Gnaeus Manlius Hilarius, Camp Praefect of the Thirteenth Legion, hereby appoint you, Lucius Lucretius Strabo, in the name of the Senate and the People of Rome, as a *frumentarius* attached to the headquarter of the said Legion. May you serve with Honor and cover yourself in Glory. *Ave* Caesar!"

Strabo returned the salute, feeling a strange sentiment he later identified as pride.

Hilarius continued, "Considering your past service to the Empire, your new rank will be the equivalent of legionary *tesserarius* with all its benefits—750 *denarii* yearly salary, eligibility for Imperial donatives, access to the legionary doctors, and so on."

"Whew," Strabo whistled. "You are too good to me, *Praefecte.*"

"Your first mission is to find out who killed Poplicola, how it was done, and why it was done. Every morning, at the first hour of the day, you'll report to me in this very office until instructed otherwise. You have a maximum of three days to close the case—we need to wrap this up before election day."

"Yes, sir. Right away, sir."

"By the way, it is a public investigation—my secretary will issue your authorization document on Legate Geta's behalf, so even the *duumviri* can't refuse to cooperate."

"Understood, sir. The people should be reassured that we take the case seriously."

Strabo saluted and turned to leave.

"One more thing, Strabo," Hilarius called after him. "If, gods forbid, Geta or his Imperial Brother are behind this, frame somebody else for the crime, will you?"

III. Tears Don't Lie

By the time Strabo got the official papers confirming his appointment, the late morning sun was more than halfway to its summit.

He walked the busy *cardo* in a dream-like state, slowly digesting the morning's events.

I could use a drink; it should help digestion. Strabo had the ideal place in mind.

A couple of blocks south of the Procurator's Office, there was a *popina* in good standing just before the Old Forum. Given its proximity, the place was popular with those whose lives revolved around the city center. However, being an establishment for respectable citizens, the local politicians and officeholders avoided it. It was favored by other, comparably harmless, forum-based parasites—pickpockets, fake jewelry salesmen, con artists of all sorts, and prostitutes.

My kind of place.

As he sat down on a rickety stool at one of the corner tables, Strabo noted the place was already half full. He ordered a flagon of the house's white wine, some olives, and cheese to munch on.

"*Frumentarius* Strabo." He mouthed the words for the first time, and they tasted sweet.

Strabo poured a cup, raising it to his mouth. He checked himself, placed the cup back on the table, and added a good measure of water.

"To your health, Praefect Hilarius! May all your psychopathic dreams come true."

After finishing the celebratory ceremony, Strabo drew a mental action plan.

Despite what Hilarius said about the loving couple, spouses were likely to kill one another. He could imagine countless motives for a conjugal crime ranging from jealousy to loud snoring. Strabo distinctly remembered his murderous fantasies when he had to share the tent with seven other legionaries.

Next, he decided to interview the running mate, Furius Mus. As improbable a killer as he might be, Strabo couldn't miss the opportunity to meet the city's most unmemorable person. In the worst-case scenario, he would forget him soon after their meeting.

Strabo planned to keep the best for last—*duumvir* Verres, host of the ominous dinner party and one of the city's chief magistrates for the year.

Aurelia Sexta, here I come!

******

Poplicola's house was southwest of the New Forum. It was only a block away from the homes of the truly rich and powerful, and still, it wasn't close enough to place the former candidate amongst the elite.

The entrance was on a narrow side street east of the vegetable market, the *holitorium*. The wind carried the smell of rotten fruits and vegetables mixed with the stench of the animals sold and slaughtered at the nearby cattle market.

"Poplicola," the red graffiti painted on the door announced.

The spaces flanking the entrances of Roman houses usually served as shops, but in this case, they were shuttered. *Business wasn't good for Poplicola.*

He ran one hand through his hair, making sure everything was in order. Then, Strabo arranged his eyepatch before using the bronze door knocker. Knock, knock, knock.

After a few heartbeats, the oak door cracked open, a skinny slave in his early thirties peering out.

"May I help you?" Skinny said timidly.

Strabo cleared his throat, then introduced himself. "My name is Lucius Lucretius Strabo, *Frumentarius* of the *Legio XIII Gemina*. I was charged to investigate the death of Cominius Pontius Poplicola."

The slave stared at him incomprehensibly.

"Is the *Domina* at home?" Strabo said.

"Yes, sir, but she is not receiving visitors currently."

"Nonetheless, I must talk to her. It is related to her husband's death." Seeing the signs of an internal struggle on the poor fellow's face, Strabo said, "Take me to her now!"

The door opened, and Strabo entered the *fauces*; the entry corridor led to the house's modest *atrium*. Since the body of Poplicola was not yet laid in state, Strabo guessed the corpse was still with the *libitinarii*, the guild of the undertakers.

The *atrium*'s center was occupied by the customary water basin, the *compluvium*, regularly fed by rainwater through the rectangular opening in the ceiling—the *impluvium*. Strabo could see the different cubicles serving as bedrooms or storage places on the wings. The few slaves needed to run a household this size were living upstairs, most probably.

He noticed the *lararium* with its shrine dedicated to the household gods—two *lares* but no sign of a famous forefather's *genius*.

Poplicola would have been the first Pontius to be elected to high office.

The plastered walls were painted red, black, and gold, a testament to the owners' good tastes. However, the lack of expensive decorations, frescos, and statues was yet another indication of a strained budget. Poplicola had no rental income, rich inheritance, or famous ancestor.

I wonder how he could afford an electoral campaign.

Beyond the small pool, Strabo could see the *tablinum* with its elevated dais and the *paterfamilias'* desk facing the entrance—it was where Poplicola conducted business, like meeting his clients and other visitors.

Behind the *tablinum* was an undecorated wall—no peristyle garden, not even a tiny *hortus*.

Presumably, the kitchen and the *latrina* were to the left of the *tablinum*, while on the right, Strabo expected to find the *triclinium*, the dining room.

By all indications, the house was a palace compared to Strabo's miserable hole, but it was only a notch above Aquilina's first-floor tenement apartment. For an aristocratic *eques*, Poplicola lived rather humbly.

"Wait here, sir," Skinny said, then walked to one of the cubicles, peered beyond the curtains, and exchanged a few hushed words with the person inside. The slave nodded and turned back towards Strabo.

"Please follow me, sir."

Strabo was led to the dining room, which was, as suspected, next to the office. There were three couches placed around a rectangular table.

"Can I bring you anything, sir? Wine? Water? Maybe some fruits?"

The Pontii might not be rich, but they were definitely well-behaved.

"No, thank you." Strabo dropped down on one of the couches.

Aurelia Sexta appeared shortly. She greeted him with a curt nod and lay on the couch opposite, facing the ceiling.

Her long raven hair was unkempt, a sign that she was tearing at it in sorrow, while her blue eyes were red after hours of crying. Despite her current state, Strabo could see she was an attractive woman. And she was obviously in pain.

Hilarius might have been right.

"My name is Lucret—" he said.

"What do you want?" She cut him off without even looking at him.

"I am investigating your husband's suspicious death."

Aurelia turned her head to face Strabo, pure hatred on her face. "Suspicious?" She sat up. "Suspicious?!?"

Strabo tensed, ready to jump up and leave at the first signs of an incoming assault. But, instead, Aurelia leaned forward and said, "These bastards poisoned my husband. That is not a suspicion." She spat the words. "But a fact!"

He tried to strike a light, neutral tone. "Can you describe what happened after your husband's return from dinner?"

"Who are you again?"

He tried to introduce himself once more. "I am Lucre—"

"I don't care about your bloody name!" She sighed deeply, trying to calm herself. "Who are you working for? Who asked you to investigate?"

"The Camp Praefect of the Thirteenth Legion," he said.

Aurelia stared at him for a couple of heartbeats. Then she shook her head. "I don't understand. I don't understand." Finally, she burst into tears, turning her back to him. And she cried and cried, her whole body shaking.

The only thing Strabo could do was wait.

After a while, Aurelia ran out of tears, and her body stopped shaking. The silence was interrupted only by her occasional sobs.

"Let me try to explain, madam," Strabo whispered.

She was startled to hear his voice. "Are you still here?" Aurelia turned her head toward him.

"I need to find out what happened, madam."

Her face in her hands, Aurelia rocked back and forth.

"I was authorized to investigate your husband's poisoning. I am a *frumentarius*, working under Camp Praefect Hilarius— he is in Sarmizegetusa to maintain order during the elections season." Strabo waited for a reaction. No reply came, so he continued, "According to your earlier statement, your husband returned from dinner circa an hour after sundown. Is this correct?"

"Yes," came the muffled reply.

It is a start.

"Did he eat or drink anything after his return?"

She pushed her hair back so Strabo could see her face. "No, nothing. He came straight to bed."

"I see. Did Pontius Poplicola tell you anything about the dinner?"

"He was angry. According to Cominius, they wanted him to withdraw from the race."

"Who are they?"

"The *duumviri* and the other bigwigs," she said. "Look, I don't know much about politics; I never cared." Aurelia shrugged. "I wanted Cominius to be happy, so I supported him as best as I could. If you want to know more about what happened at the dinner, please ask Gaius."

"Gaius?"

"Yes, my husband's friend and running partner, Gaius Furius Mus."

Mental face slap! How could I forget about him?

Strabo prompted gently. "What happened next?"

"Well, it was late, and we went to sleep. I remember Cominius woke me up at some point during the night, complaining about tingling in his throat and mouth. After that, I fell asleep again." She paused, struggling to keep herself together. "I woke up later, and Cominius was not in bed. I called out, but there was no answer, so I rose. And there he was…," sob, "motionless, on the *latrina*…his eyes open, foam at his mouth…." A renewed wave of crying shook her body.

Strabo sat patiently, not knowing what else to do. He couldn't just walk out on her, although he probably won't obtain any additional piece of information.

"I am sorry for your loss, madam," he said eventually. "Any idea where I can find Mus?"

"Oh, poor Gaius, he must be at the *basilica*, seeking justice for Cominius. He was always so loyal ever since we were children."

"You grew up together, then?"

"Yes." She smiled weakly. "Cominius was always involved in one of his big schemes, and Mus was always there to get him out of trouble."

"What about you, madam?"

"What about me? I was hopelessly in love with Cominius from an early age, supporting him unconditionally. Poor Gaius, he tried to talk me out of following Cominius' crazy schemes but to no avail."

"I see. Thank you again for your time." Strabo rose to leave.

"Love is all-powerful, Strabo. It can make you do things you'd never thought yourself capable of."

He nodded his farewell and walked toward the entrance, followed by the sound of Aurelia's heartbroken sobs.

IV. The Unforgettable Performance

Strabo decided to go around the New Forum to avoid the midday crowds.

His journey led him up the easternmost *cardo* skirting the elite's neighborhood. There were only a few houses between the street and the city wall. The first residence he passed covered an entire city block, the tall stone enclosure hiding it from view—he could guess the luxurious palace's layout, though. Everybody knew who owned it; Aulus Hostilius Avitus, arguably the most influential man in Sarmizegetusa.

Being the incumbent *duumvir quinquennales*, Avitus held one of the highest offices in the colony. The other equivalent position was traditionally reserved for the emperor in his capacity as Perpetual Censor.

As the title suggested, the *duumvir quinquennales* was appointed by the local assembly every five years to oversee the citizen census, uphold public morality, and purge the *curia* of immoral or corrupt members. Naturally, given the nature of the office, only one with a long and impeccable public record could hold it. At least, this was the theory.

In practice, however, one had to be sleek enough to be repeatedly elected over a decades-spanning public career, rich enough to finance these recurring electoral campaigns, and intelligent enough to hide the corrupt means by which one got the necessary wealth. The palatial house and exalted office proved that Avitus embodied all three essential qualities.

As Strabo walked on, he passed a few other impressive properties—they faced a couple of high-rise tenements similar to the one he lived in.

This familiar setup made the Empire what it is today.

The elites sharing the same streets with the poor ensured the affluent officeholders were under constant public pressure—

they had to deliver or risk verbal abuse or even physical harm as soon as they left the protection of their houses.

Strabo turned left on the *decumanus* and walked to the entrance of the Old Forum—it was the city's throbbing heart. Citizens met here to socialize and gossip, listen to political speeches and public announcements, and resolve their affairs at different public institutions and agencies.

The public square's southern part housed the *basilica*, the city's main administrative building. It was where the local *curia* met, the chief magistrates held court, the public archives were kept, the city treasury was deposited, and dangerous suspects were held between the hearings.

Let's find dear Gaius.

As soon as he passed through the pillared entrance, Strabo noticed the crowd gathered to listen to a guy wearing the *toga candida*, the white garment candidates wore to symbolize their purity.

A pure politician. What a joke.

Strabo got closer to the elevated platform.

The speaker was a mouse-like creature with rare brown hair and a sweaty face. The toga was too large for his skinny body, and the squealing voice did nothing to improve his overall appearance. He was highly agitated, his spindly arms frantically moving as he tried to deliver his message. The whole scene would have been amusing if not for the seriousness of his words.

"…all he desired was to ensure the prosperity of our beloved city. He dreamed of a colony where even the poorest Roman could have a secure and dignified existence. Remember the words of Cicero, '*Of all the occupations by which gain is secured, none is better than agriculture, none more profitable, none more delightful, none more becoming to a free man.*'"

Although the delivery was far from convincing, he struck a nerve, as indicated by the murmurs of approval.

Mus pushed on, sadness in his voice, "Oh, dear Cominius, what were you thinking to take on the powers of the day all by yourself?" He paused for effect, raised his hands to the sky, and continued, "My dear, dear friend, haven't I warned you of the dark forces conspiring against us?" Mus placed his left hand on his hip while wagging the other one in a gesture of reprimand. "Alas, you wouldn't listen. You were blinded by the dream of Romans living as the founding fathers once did."

His face buried in his palms, Mus' head shook in grief. He turned his gaze back to the crowd. "I pleaded with him many times, but his answer was always the same. 'Cincinnatus worked the land before he was called to save the Republic,' he used to tell me. 'And he returned to the plow as soon as

Rome was safe again. Just imagine, *frater*, the potential of a colony inhabited by a thousand *Cincinnati*.'"

The crowd became agitated, and more and more shouts of approval echoed throughout the square.

"This was the dream of the man I loved like a brother. A *colonia* where every Roman could stand tall and proud, living the life our wise ancestors envisioned. A settlement where every citizen has the means to a dignified life. A place where every Roman could aspire to serve their fellow citizens as elected magistrates. A city where the squalid rooms of the tenements are reserved for slaves and barbarians while true Romans live the noble existence of citizen-farmers, plowing the lands surrounding our great city."

The audience drank in every word, and when Mus paused to draw his breath, Strabo could feel the tension gripping the heaving multitudes.

"Cominius Pontius Poplicola sacrificed everything to achieve this dream!" Mus thundered.

The crowd exploded. "PO-PLI-CO-LA, PO-PLI-CO-LA!"

After a while, Mus waved them to silence. "So what are we going to do about it now that Poplicola was silenced? Are we giving up on his dream?"

"NOOOOO!" the booming answer came.

"Are we going to let the blood-sucking parasites keep us in poverty?"

"NOOOOOOOO!"

"Or will we fight and fight and fight until Poplicola's dream is fulfilled?"

"FIGHT, FIGHT, FIGHT!"

Strabo caught himself cheering with the crowd, pumping the air with his right hand as he shouted for the fight to go on.

He stopped immediately, hoping Hilarius was not around to see him.

Despite his theatrics, Mus couldn't hide his astonishment at the crowd's positive reaction. He wiped his tears and declaimed as loudly and solemnly as he could, "I, Gaius Furius Mus, hereby take this solemn oath in front of the industrious citizens of *Colonia* Ulpia Traiana Sarmizegetusa. If elected as *aedile* and into the *curia*, I will fight tirelessly to ensure the surrounding public lands' distribution to the impoverished citizens of our city. May the gods give me strength!"

There was chaos as the frenzied masses shouted encouragement and approval in a cacophony of sounds.

I just witnessed the unforgettable performance of the most forgettable man in Sarmizegetusa.

Hilarius' worst fears were confirmed. If they did not find a way to clear the air as soon as possible, the ensuing bloodbath would spread far and wide, signaling the beginning of yet another civil war.

No pressure, Stinky.

******

As soon as Mus climbed down from the platform, he was surrounded by the cheering mob. While initially taken aback by his newfound popularity, Mus recovered his wits, shaking hands left and right, exchanging reassuring words here or making a promise for justice there.

Strabo elbowed his way forward and got within earshot, just behind a tightly packed group circling Mus.

"Furius Mus, I need to talk to you!" Strabo shouted to no avail. "Oi, Furius, Aurelia sent me!"

Aurelia's name piqued Mus' interest, and he paced the faces around him to identify the caller.

"I am here!" Strabo raised his hands. Then, finally, some of the people withdrew just enough for Strabo to squeeze through.

"What was that about Aurelia?" Mus said, shouting into Strabo's left ear.

"Aurelia Sexta sent me. She wants me to clarify the circumstances of Poplicola's...uh...untimely death."

Mus glanced around, reluctant to miss the opportunity to canvas a mass of acclaiming citizens. "I tell you what," he said eventually, clasping Strabo's hand. "Join me for a drink at my father's villa, just outside the eastern gate." He looked up to the sun to estimate the time. "Let's say, in a couple of hours from now." He let Strabo's hand go and moved to the next potential voter.

After shoving his way out of the crowd, Strabo decided to spend the time collecting political gossip.

As soon as he left the Old Forum, Strabo noticed a detachment of legionaries marching down the *cardo*. Hilarius led them.

"*Praefecte*, sir!" Strabo walked ahead to meet his commander.

"Strabo, what in the name of all the gods is happening? We received reports of rioting."

"There is no rioting, sir." *But you are about to provoke one*, Strabo thought. "Permission to report, sir."

Hilarius nodded.

"Gaius Furius Mus was rabble-rousing. He seems determined to proceed with his candidacy, promising to implement Poplicola's proposed land distribution if elected."

"The Mouse was rabble-rousing? That ridiculous little man?" Hilarius was unconvinced. "The binge drinking must have dulled your powers of observation."

"Sir, I heard him with my own ears. Mus implied Poplicola was eliminated because he planned to distribute land to the poor. Still, if he, Gaius Furius Mus, is elected, he'll fight for the people and bla bla bla…."

Hilarius remained skeptical. "He said all that? In so many words?"

"Yes, sir. It was a good speech, to be honest."

"And this is why the riots broke out?"

"No, sir. There were no riots."

Sorry, Gnaeus dear, no bloodbath today, maybe tomorrow if you are a good boy.

Strabo explained, "The people are aroused, but there is no looting or violence. If I may, sir, I would suggest leaving some patrols around in case some hotheads need calming. Otherwise, a show of force might only provoke the crowd."

Hilarius pondered Strabo's words—he obviously itched for a fight.

"Think of what you told me, sir. Bad news travels fast. Beating up citizens because they joined a political rally would only strengthen the anti-Emperor propaganda."

The Praefect took a calming breath, then another one and another. Then, finally, he relented. "You are right, *Frumentarie*. Beating these bastards up in broad daylight might not look good." He shook his head before saying, "I will handle things here; go about your investigation. Tomorrow at the first hour, I expect your report."

"Yes, sir."

Strabo saluted and returned to his gossip-collecting mission.

V. The Cup of Wisdom

The street in front of the *Cucuculus* was already packed. People living in the nearby *insulae* gathered in groups discussing the day's events while they savored the dubious wine.

Strabo fetched a cup from the bartender. He wasn't recognized, given his new, honorable look. Then, while searching for familiar faces, he noticed Porcius' disheveled shape walking away from the tavern. Strabo followed him for a short distance until Porcius stopped in front of one of the tenement walls, pulled up his tunic, and peed. Strabo waited patiently, and when he judged Porcius was almost done, he put a heavy hand on his victim's shoulder.

"*Salve*, citizen!"

"It wasn't me! I didn't do it!" Porcius jumped and raised his hands defensively, expecting to be clobbered for his unsanitary deed.

Strabo couldn't keep a straight face and exploded in laughter. "Calm down, Porcius. It is me, Strabo."

"Squinty Stinky?" Porcius' eyes were wide open when he finally recognized his drinking mate. "Oh, no, you were serious about visiting the *Procurator*'s Office, weren't you?"

"Yes, I was."

"I know you were desperate and all, but to scoop so low…."

"Look, *frater*, the pay is good, and there are many fringe benefits."

"Fringe benefits, he says." Porcius cackled. "I bet there are."

"Yes, there are. And if you really want to know, I am enjoying this job," a slightly offended Strabo said.

"Okay, okay, don't be so touchy; I get it. We all do what we have to. But, still, to be the *Procurator*'s bum-boy…"

"What?!? What the hell are you talking about, you disgusting pig?" Strabo's face was red, and he had to apply all his self-control to avoid beating Porcius to a pulp.

"Well, it is common knowledge that the *Procurator* fancies young boys. You are a bit older, still…."

"I am not the fucking *Procurator*'s fucking bum-boy, you miserable excuse of a man. I was appointed as a *frumentarius* attached to the Gemina's HQ."

Porcius looked at Strabo, doubt on his face. "Squinty Stinky, the Secret Agent? How the mighty legions have fallen." He laughed his horrible laugh, wet cough and all, and then he saw an opportunity. "So you came to celebrate with your old buddy? Such a nice fellow, my friend Stinky."

"Fuck off, Porcius. I came to pick your dirty brain. Answer me well, and you are looking forward to a memorable night. That is to say, you'll be so drunk that you'll remember shit come the morning." Observing Porcius' toothless grin was as discomforting as ever—at least he was willing to cooperate.

"What do you want to know, *Domine*?"

"Who is supporting Varro and Lentulus for *aedile*-ship and why?"

Porcius pointed to the wall he soiled earlier, and Strabo noticed a few lines of black graffiti. It read, '*Please elect Varro and Lentulus for aediles. If you meanly blot this message out, I hope you catch something nasty. Aquilina.*'

"Why would Aquilina give a shit about the election?" Strabo said.

Porcius sighed. "Stinky the Spy, what a joke. Look, I will explain everything, but my throat is dry."

Strabo offered his cup, crossed his arms, and said, "I am listening."

"Poplicola's main campaign promise was land distribution to the poor—even you must have heard about that." Strabo nodded. "If the poor get the land, many will move out of the city proper and build farms around Sarmizegetusa." Porcius waited for a couple of heartbeats hoping Strabo would eventually catch on. When he didn't, Porcius continued, "There will be nobody to rent the shitholes at the top of those nasty apartment buildings. Aquilina and her ilk will have no choice but to rent to slaves, freedmen, and barbarians. Rental prices will plummet, and the rich parasites will lose money."

"Aha, now I get it."

"Not the sharpest blade in the legions, are you?"

"Fine, but what about Governor Geta? What does he have against land distribution? Surely the Emperor's brother and our noble *honestiores* don't care about the woes of the likes of Aquilina."

"No, they don't. The gentry might even enjoy watching as the wealthier plebs become poorer. It is why they supported Poplicola and his mousy friend at the beginning. However, Legate Geta pointed out the error of their ways. He reminded them how our beloved Emperor Severus obtained his exalted position with the support of countless legions. Many of those legionaries are now due to receive their *praemia*, land allotment included. You got one, too, right? Where is your plot?"

"Yes, I did. It is a few miles north of here."

"See? There are 30.000 more veterans in line to get theirs. And what better place to distribute a potential reserve force than the empty lands surrounding the metropolis of a border province? Remember the Iazyges? The Quadi? The Marcomanni?"

Strabo slapped his face so hard his eyepatch almost fell off. "Fuck me. How did I not see it?"

Porcius nodded approvingly. "I was wondering the same thing. How could the *Gemina*'s best not see the obvious?" He laughed out loud.

Strabo summarized his understanding, "The Emperor needs the land for his veterans, so he is against Poplicola's plan. The wealthy plebs who own the apartment buildings want to secure their income, so they are against Poplicola's plan. So are the tavern owners, the fullers, the barbers, and all the mid-level *humiliores* who cater to the hungry, thirsty, unwashed masses."

"Who is unwashed?" Porcius bristled, looking over his miserable tunic.

Strabo ignored him. "By their nature, the *honestiores* are constantly competing for Imperial favor. Most of them switched their support to Geta's candidates despite their desire to see the well-off plebs being put down a notch.

Eventually, they all lined up behind Varro and Lentulus and against Poplicola and Mus."

"Spot on, Stinky."

This Poplicola guy had more enemies than Emperor Severus.

"But how could a humble *aedile* accomplish the land distribution all by himself?" Strabo said.

"How the fuck should I know? Do I look like a member of the *curia* to you?"

No, Porcius didn't look like a *decurion* to Strabo—he lacked the devious political mind, among other things.

VI. The Greasy Pole

Strabo picked up the pace as he left through the city's eastern gate. The sky was cloudy, and one of those sudden summer rains was in the making. He hoped to find Furius Mus' father's villa before the downpour.

The suburbs of the east were the domain of the *homo novus*, the new man, people who acquired their wealth and status recently without the benefit of a long line of distinguished ancestors. They were rich enough to build sumptuous villas outside the city. Still, they weren't *old* enough to have acquired a palatial *domus* in the city proper—even if they could afford one, the long-established families were reluctant to sell their prestigious spots nested within the city's walls.

Mus' father was one Gaius Furius Mulio. His nickname indicated the source of his riches—the mules. Mulio started as a simple muleteer, but his luck turned when he weathered the destruction of the Marcomannic invasion unscathed. With most of his competitors dead or otherwise indisposed, Mulio provided pack animals for the gold mines of Alburnus Maior—those mountains had a lot of gold, and many mules were needed to transport it to the Imperial mints. Thus, the elderly Furius went from rags to riches in a couple of short years. These days, he provided animals to most caravans and mule trains crisscrossing the province of *Tres Daciae*.

Strabo reached the gates of Mulio's extensive estate as soon as the first drops fell. A paved tree-lined path led to the enormous villa, linden trees sheltering Strabo from the summer rain.

He used the bronze knocker of the impressive oak gate to signal his arrival—a well-dressed middle-aged slave answered. If Strabo hadn't known better, he might have mistaken the dignified man for a Roman senator. He had carefully trimmed silver hair, his tall body straight, and his posture proud. He held his imposing nose high, barely acknowledging the unassuming guest.

"Can I help you, sir?" Snooty said.

"My name is Lucius Lucretius Strabo. I am here on the invitation of Gaius Furius Mus," Strabo said in the most confident tone he could muster. *I will not let a slave intimidate me.*

"Is that so?" Snooty sniffed, weighing Strabo methodically from head to toe.

I hope my tunic is not crumpled.

Snooty finished his inspection with another sniff. "Please come in, sir. Wait in the *atrium* while I inform the young master of your arrival."

Well, this was an atrium, all right.

It hosted a huge *compluvium* in its center that was more like a man-made lake than a pool. The water's surface bubbled because of the pouring rain. There were countless cubicles on the sides, each of them probably larger than Strabo's room at Aquilina's.

Beyond the imposing desk of the *tablinum*, Strabo could see parts of a large peristyle garden the size of an average public park in Rome.

Mus appeared from one of the cubicles on the left, Snooty in tow.

"Good to see you again, *amice*. Aurelia's friends are my friends." They clasped each other's forearms in the traditional Roman handshake. "Welcome to our humble abode."

"Thank you, Furius Mus, for seeing me. Is there somewhere we could talk?" Strabo said, discreetly nodding towards Snooty.

"Ah, don't worry about Hercules. I would trust him with my life." Mus smiled. "Actually, I trust him with my life since he runs every aspect of our household."

"I see." It was the only comment Strabo could force himself to make.

"But where are my manners? Please come in and join me for a snack."

He led Strabo to a spacious dining room with comfortable couches on three sides; a platter of fruits and sweetmeats was already on the table.

They sat on opposing couches.

"We haven't been properly introduced, I am afraid. While you know who I am, I am at a disadvantage." The fake charm of a second-rate politician oozed from Mus' every word.

Now I see why Hilarius tries to forget the man.

"My name is Lucius Lucretius Strabo. I am a *frumentarius* working for Camp Praefect Hilarius of *Legio XIII Gemina.* Since the Praefect was deputized to the *Procurator's Office* to ensure orderly elections, he directed me to investigate the circumstances of your former colleague's untimely demise." *I can use fancy talk, too.*

"Ah, I thought Aurelia Sexta sent you." Mus seemed disappointed.

"She did," Strabo said. "Aurelia specifically asked me to talk to you and elucidate the circumstances of her husband's death."

"Well, it shouldn't be too hard to figure it out. Cominius was poisoned during our dinner at *Duumvir* Verres' place."

"What makes you say that? Maybe it was food poisoning, so he might not have been deliberately murdered," Strabo said.

"Let me try to break this down for you, *Frumentarie*. Cominius and I spent the whole day at the Old Forum, canvassing for the election. No food or drink was consumed other than water from the fountains. We were about to call it a day when one of Verres' slaves invited us to his house for dinner. We went, ate, drank, talked, and returned home. Aurelia later told me that poor Cominius went straight to bed, got sick at night, and was found dead in the morning. On the latrine." He shook his head sadly. "What a way to die for such a gifted young man."

They stood in respectful silence for a while, and Mus finally said, "As you can see, *Frumentarie*, the only time Cominius could have consumed something poisonous was at the dinner. Nobody else got sick, so we can probably rule out food poisoning."

Mus' whole demeanor was somehow wrong. The succinct way he presented the facts seemed out of place. It was not how somebody would describe the murder of his best friend.

Perhaps it is his way of dealing with grief. Each person reacted differently to sudden shock.

"Before we jump to conclusions, I would like to inquire about the dinner. Who was present?"

"Suit yourself, *Frumentarie*. Both *duumviri*—Verres and Aculeo—were there. The current *aediles* Macula and Merula also attended in addition to our electoral rivals, Varro and Lentulus."

"No one else?"

"*Quinquennales* Avitus dropped by for a quick word, but he didn't stay for the whole evening."

"I see. May I inquire about the topic of the night?" Strabo said.

"I guess it is no secret, given your position. They tried to persuade us to withdraw from the election."

"And why was that?"

"Were you not listening in the forum today? Cominius was adamant about distributing land to Sarmizegetusa's impoverished citizens. Verres and his gang were livid, afraid to antagonize our beloved Legate and Imperial Baby Brother."

"Please excuse my lack of knowledge, Furius Mus, but even if elected, how could a mere *aedile* implement the land distribution against the wishes of the *curia*?"

"Two, not one," Mus said in a small voice.

"I beg your pardon?"

"Two mere *aediles*, not one. I was on the ticket, too, you know."

Somebody was not happy living in his friend's shadow.

Strabo made a mental note and said, "Of course, how could two *aediles* implement this all by themselves?"

"They couldn't," Mus said. "Not without the *curia*'s support." Mus popped a sweetmeat into his mouth and continued, "Whoever gets elected *aedile* gets a seat in the *curia*, right? Membership is for life unless one is expelled by the *quinquennales* for immorality or falling into poverty."

Strabo noded. "Being elected as *aedile* comes with a lifelong membership in the big boys club. It also opens the path for a military career and the subsequent lucrative positions in the imperial administration."

"Exactly," Mus said. "More so, only a former *aedile* can run for one of the two top executive positions of *duumvir*. Since the number of *aediles* is limited to two per year and the outgoing *duumviri* can't run again for ten years, the *aediles* for the current year are almost guaranteed to be elected as next year's *duumviri*." Mus was in his element explaining all this. There was a hint of pride in his voice.

Could he have been the mastermind behind Poplicola's plan?

"First *aediles* and lifelong decurions, next *duumviri*—this part is clear." Strabo scratched his head. "I still don't see how the two of you could get the land distribution bill through a hostile assembly."

Mus smiled. "You would be astonished by the sheer number of decurions secretly supporting our initiative. They are reluctant to display their views publicly, but if someone else would put forward the land distribution bill, they might vote for it." Mus was amused at Strabo's confused expression. "Politicians are pack animals, my dear Strabo. They are cowards individually but are ferocious when amid their pack. At the very least, they could block any alternative bills until a friendlier political climate would return to our city. If you want to delay a legislative initiative indefinitely, the best course of action is to create a *curiate* commission to analyze it." He grinned. "Are you following, *Frumentarie?*"

"Yes, the key was for you two to be inducted into the *curia*. Then, one way or another, you could have blocked Governor Geta's initiative to distribute the land to Emperor Severus' veterans while building support for your own bill." Strabo nodded. "Very smart, I must say."

Let's massage his ego a bit.

"Smart indeed." Mus beamed with pride. "Even if we couldn't gather enough support next year, we would have been elected *duumviri* the year after, and we could have supported a similarly minded duo to succeed us as *aediles*." He gazed into the middle distance, relishing their prospective success. "Cominius and I would be the *duumviri*, two of our supporters would be *aediles*, and Legate Geta would probably be reassigned to his next provincial posting by then. Without the Governor's opposition, our leverage in the *curia* would have been strong enough to gather a majority for our plans."

Strabo nodded in genuine admiration. Whoever planned this had a sound mind for intrigue. "And you think Pontius Poplicola was poisoned to derail your plans."

"Obviously," Mus said.

"Why wouldn't they poison both of you, then? Your earlier performance in the forum proved that killing Poplicola wasn't enough to stop your initiative."

Mus smiled bitterly. "Always ignored, always underestimated. The story of my life."

"Hearing your speech today, I would say they ignored you at their own peril." *I will certainly not repeat the same mistake*, Strabo thought, but said instead, "One curiosity, though, if you don't mind me asking."

"Go ahead. If I mind, I will not answer."

"Why are you supporting this initiative? I mean, your father is a rich man. Why risk your comfortable future, even your life, by antagonizing the Emperor? *Curia* or not, Severus could march his troops into the forum and get all of you arrested and executed. The days of the Republic are long gone."

Mus stared at Strabo for a while, his eyes weighing him shrewdly. "There is such a thing as patriotism," he eventually said. "I am ready to sacrifice my life for the good of my fellow citizens." He raised his chin in a somewhat failed attempt to project dignity.

He is so full of it!

"The veterans of Severus' legions are patriots, too; they risked their lives for the Empire. I lost an eye at Lugdunum, you know," Strabo said, pointing to his eyepatch.

"I am sorry, *Frumentarie*; I didn't mean to minimize the sacrifices made by our fighting men. However, there is enough land to the north to accommodate the veterans. Napoca, Apulum, and Potaissa come to mind."

"Why do you think Legate Geta chose Sarmizegetusa to settle the veterans instead of the other colonies?"

"Who knows? There might be competing interests in the other colonies, or Geta might have promised the lands there to his cronies. I honestly don't know. What I do know is that Sarmizegetusa's citizens need those plots to be prosperous."

"To change the subject entirely, you, Cominius, and Aurelia are childhood friends. Am I correct?"

"Yes, you are. We have known each other since early childhood."

"Aurelia Sexta seems very fond of you. She recounted how you always cared for her and tried to keep Cominius out of trouble."

Mus smiled a natural, genuine smile, not the politician's smirk. "Dear Aurelia, she is such a gentle soul. I did my best to protect her from the fallout of Cominius' different schemes."

"This is what true friends are for," Strabo said. "Cominius got in trouble often, didn't he?"

Mus laughed. "That is an understatement, my dear fellow. To understand what made Cominius tick, you need to be aware of his background. Although an honorable one, his family struggled with money for as long as I can remember. The situation bothered Cominius a lot—even as a teenager. He always dreamed of reaching the top and improving his family's fortunes." Mus paused, then added, "There is nothing wrong with ambition, mind you. Every self-respecting Roman has to try to achieve glory and fame for his family."

"Indeed, there is nothing wrong with that. Jumping back to the present, running an electoral campaign requires money. If Poplicola wasn't well off, how could he afford it?"

"A friend in need is a friend indeed. Am I right, *Frumentarie*?" Mus spread his arms. "As you can see, my father can afford to support me, and, in turn, I can afford to support my best friend."

Who was helping whom, I wonder? Mus by paying for the campaign or the popular Poplicola by sharing the ticket with unelectable Mus?

"Your devotion is admirable, Furius Mus. Poplicola was truly a blessed man to have friends like you. Still, there are cheaper ways to kick-start a good career. It wasn't necessary to be elected to political office. Poplicola could have served as a priest and then joined the army as the commander of an auxiliary unit. Eventually, he could have become a *Procurator*, earning a lot of money and gaining social status. Who knows, he might have made it all the way up to the governorship of Egypt."

Mus shrugged. "Cominius desired money and social status, but he also wished to serve his fellow citizens. Running for *aedile*-ship was as much about his personal ambition as it was about the good of Sarmizegetusa."

"What about Aurelia? Why was she supporting Poplicola's endeavors? Was her family struggling as well?"

"No, Aurelia's family is content with their lot. Her father is a rather prosperous individual. He is a wheat importer, you see. With the recent civil strife following on the back of the previous Marcommanic invasion, our province is not self-sufficient yet, as you may know. One more reason to distribute land to the poor."

"But wouldn't Poplicola's plan undermine his father-in-law's business? If we could produce enough grain in the province, there wouldn't be a need to import it anymore."

"He could always switch to exporting, I guess. But, to be honest, I never thought about it."

"Of course, but I can't understand why Aurelia would support him in all his schemes—even as children?" Strabo scratched his head.

"Isn't it obvious? She was in love. Utterly. Madly. Blindly. She would have followed him to the gates of Hades if he asked."

"Now I understand. It is why you had to protect her even from herself. You are truly an amazing friend, Furius Mus. If only I would have the good fortune of Aurelia and Cominius, I might be a centurion by now."

Was this flattery too much? No, he seems to bask in it. He probably wasn't accustomed to being the center of attention. He was usually in the shadow of his more popular friend.

Strabo continued, "Why not talk Cominius out of his more spurious plans?"

"He wouldn't listen once he set his mind to something. Instead, he charged ahead without considering the misfortune he could bring onto himself or the others around him."

"That attitude doesn't sound very friend-like," Strabo said.

Mus nodded initially, but then he smelled the trap and checked himself. "I don't like where this conversation is going, Lucretius Strabo. Cominius was my friend, and I helped him as much as I could and tried to protect Aurelia in the process."

"I apologize. I didn't mean to imply anything inappropriate."
And now for the final gamble… "I am pained to note your failure to protect Aurelia despite your best efforts. It must have been difficult for you to digest."

"What do you mean?"

"Well, her husband died because of his latest scheme. And you supported him wholeheartedly instead of protecting her as usual. If only you could have talked him out of his plans, he might still be alive today, satisfying Aurelia."

"She is safe and sound, is she not?" Mus said coldly.

"Yes, she is finally safe now that Poplicola is not around anymore to put her into harm's way," Strabo said.

Mus stood up abruptly. "I think you overstayed your welcome, *Frumentarie* Strabo. I have answered all your questions. Now I am asking you to leave."

That went well, Strabo thought as his new friend, Snooty,

ushered him out.

VII. Midnight Musings

Strabo studied the ceiling of his room in the yellow light of the oil lamp. *What a day.*

He lay on his bed, the new one he had bought the previous afternoon. Strabo also acquired a new feather-stuffed mattress, a small dining table, a couple of stools, a proper chamber pot, a cupboard, and an oak trunk to store his clothing and personal belongings. The room was almost homey. Even the cockroaches had moved out now that Strabo had cleaned it.

"Let's summarize our findings so far," he said out loud.

Aurelia was grief-stricken, and Strabo was convinced her pain was genuine—she couldn't have faked it so well. Mus corroborated her account of being deeply in love with Poplicola and her habit of blindly following her husband, irrespective of how dubious his schemes might have been.

What motives could a loving, supporting wife have to murder her husband?

Admittedly, Strabo's experience with love was limited. Still, based on the information at his disposal, he couldn't think of a motive, at least not for now.

Mus, on the other hand, could have had multiple motives.

Based on their conversation, Strabo believed Mus had been secretly in love with Aurelia since childhood. He openly admitted to shielding her from Poplicola's risky decisions' fallout, and he even seemed relieved Aurelia was out of danger now that her husband had passed away.

Another motive could have been Mus' not-so-well-hidden bitterness of constantly living in his friend's shadow. After all, he devised the political scheme that could have propelled both of them to the very top of society. He was the one financing the whole endeavor. It was reasonable for Mus to expect at least a bit of recognition instead of being fully eclipsed by Poplicola. With Poplicola out of the way, Mus finally had the chance to shine, and he did shine, as Strabo had witnessed earlier.

Cui bono? To whom is it a benefit?

Mus had ample motive by Cicero's measure. With Poplicola out of the way, Mus could dominate the political stage. He got the target of his secret affections out of harm's way, and, who knows, Aurelia might even recognize him for the loyal and caring friend he has always been and eventually reciprocate his feelings.

Mus also had the opportunity to poison Poplicola. He was there during the ominous dinner at Verres' house. Still, being in the same room simultaneously didn't prove anything. Did Mus and Poplicola sit at the same table? What about the kitchen? Did Mus have access to it? *I definitely need to interview Verres for more details.*

Last but not least, motive and opportunity were insufficient unless Mus had the means to execute the foul dead. What kind of poison was used? Was it administered through the food or the drinks?

Even assuming Mus had motives, opportunity, and means, Poplicola could just as easily have been poisoned by one of his political rivals.

Well, there is a long day ahead of us.

Strabo sighed, blowing out the lamp.

VIII. The Spices of Life and Death

Strabo finished his light breakfast at a *taberna* nearby Aquilina's tenement.

He reported to Hilarius in the morning, as instructed. Needless to say, the old tyrant was not happy with his progress. The pressure to clear the air before Furius Mus could further stoke the people's anger mounted with every passing day; the elections were only four days away. So after Hilarius took out his frustration on Strabo, he let him return to his task.

Judging Verres to be busy receiving his clients for the morning *salutatio*, Strabo decided to look into the substance used on Poplicola.

He crossed the *decumanus* and headed northward. He knew of a store peddling concoctions and remedies, an apothecary of sorts. Once Strabo found the place, he entered. The air was heavy with the smell of the various herbs. He noticed the owner standing behind the counter.

"Welcome," the witch said. "What can old Livia do for a young man such as you? You are looking for a love potion, aren't you?" She grinned, her black and rotten teeth barely visible in the dimly lit shop.

Strabo shook his head. "Not exactly."

"Ah, I see." She cackled. "You have problems…down there. Such a pity for a youngster, but nothing Auntie Livia can't heal."

"Nothing of the sort, I assure you." Strabo blushed and then added quickly, before the horrid creature could come up with more guesses, "I am looking for wisdom."

She giggled. "Aren't we all? Try the philosophers in the forum."

Strabo took a silver *denarius* from his purse and said, "And here I was, ready to part with this shiny coin."

"What do you want to know?"

"Tickling of the mouth and throat followed by vomiting, diarrhea, and eventual death. What kind of poison could cause this?"

"Nothing can cause that. At least not for one measly *denarius*." She grinned shrewdly.

"Argh, what about two *denarii*?"

"Make it three. My memory is not what it used to be, you see."

"Fine, just talk already."

"*Colchicum autumnale*, the autumn crocus. The first symptoms kick in a couple of hours after ingestion, tickling of the mouth and throat, usually followed by vomiting and diarrhea. Next, slow paralysis sets in, eventually leading to suffocation and death. The whole process can take up to six hours. Horrible way to die, I must tell you."

"Is it easy to procure?"

"It grows all over the place. I would say you can find it at most herbalists. Not here, mind you. Unless…" She flashed another rotten grin.

Strabo put the coins on the counter. "Good to know. Thank you for your assistance."

Once he was back on the sunny street, Strabo drew a deep breath to clear his lungs of the rich aroma of the shop.

A couple of hours, she said.

Poplicola couldn't be poisoned before dinner; this much was clear now. According to Aurelia, her husband felt sick sometimes after falling asleep—it must have been at least one hour after Poplicola left Verres' house.

If nothing else, the herbalist dispelled any lingering doubts about the time of the murder. It had happened around dinner time, definitely not earlier. Also, the poisoning was deliberate so Strabo could eliminate food poisoning as a cause of death.

It's time to visit Verres.

IX. The Dinner Arrangements

Verres' house was on the same street as *Quinquennales* Avitus' sumptuous villa, although more modest in comparison since it occupied only half a city block. The home of a former *duumvir* occupied the other half.

Strabo was in the *atrium*, a dozen lesser clients also waiting for an audience with their patron. He presented his credentials to one of Verres' slaves and was asked to wait until the *duumvir* was ready to see him.

Having nothing else to do, Strabo had a closer look at the *lararium*.

Veres was from a distinguished line of decurions. It seemed the Terentii had at least one duumvir in each generation from when *Colonia* Ulpia Traiana Sarmizegetusa was founded almost a century ago. Surprisingly, though, none of them embarked on a career path in the wider imperial world. Veres' ancestors preferred to be the big fishes in a small pond. Or maybe they weren't eager to suffer through a decade of military service. *Who could blame them?*

The *secretarius* finally returned, bowed slightly, and asked Strabo to follow him. They went through the *atrium* to an office fitting one of the city's two senior magistrates.

Verres was a fat man in his fifties. His receding hairline showed his age as opposed to his wrinkle-free fat face, which made him look younger and jovial. However, as soon as he opened his mouth, the illusion of good humor was utterly shattered.

"Look, Strabo, I don't have time for this nonsense. Legate Geta might have authorized you to investigate, but please make it as brief as possible. I am a busy man."

Busy feeding your colossal belly.

"I understand, *Duumvir* Verres; I'll do my best. However, I assumed you would appreciate a thorough investigation before we'd start pointing fingers. The murder happened in your home, after all." Strabo smiled inwardly. *Chew on that, fatso!*

"W-w-what are you talking about? Pointing fingers? Murder?" Fatso was sweating now, and his arrogance had disappeared as if by magic.

Strabo continued, "Indeed, all the evidence points to a premeditated murder. The evolution of the symptoms places the poisoning around the time the late Poplicola was dining at your house."

"I beg your pardon! If you are implying that I was…"

Strabo cut the protestations curtly. "I am not implying anything, *Duumvir*. It is for Legate Geta to judge. My job is to provide the Governor with an accurate picture." This time Strabo couldn't hide his polite but malicious smile.

Verres was flustered but eventually got himself together and put on a more dignified face. "Then let's make sure our beloved Legate has all the necessary information."

That's better.

Strabo sat uninvited, opened his clay tablet holder, and pretended to run through some notes. "Could you please tell me more about the dinner? I understand you sent one of your slaves to the forum, inviting Pontius Poplicola and Furius Mus to dinner. Is that right?"

"It was more like confirming an appointment requested by Poplicola," Verres said sourly.

"What do you mean by that?" Strabo said, trying to hide his surprise.

"Why do I always get the stupid ones?" Verres rolled his eyes; his arrogant self was back. He signaled his *secretarius.* "Bring me some snacks. I have a feeling this will be a long discussion." He turned to Strabo and sighed. "Why do you think Poplicola chose to run on the land distribution platform?"

"Because it was a popular topic with the *humiliores*. He knew he had a high chance to be elected," Strabo said, worried not to miss something important.

"Oh, really?" Verres said mockingly. "And then what? Let's assume he would have been elected. What then?"

"Well, he would have fought tooth and nail to get the distribution done."

Verres shook his head, the fat jowls wagging almost obscenely. "You are even more unimaginative than I expected. Do you honestly believe a nobody from a gods-forsaken province would stop Emperor Severus from rewarding his veterans?" Verres looked at Strabo questioningly. When no answer was forthcoming, he continued, "No, sonny. Poplicola had no chance to push the land distribution through, and he knew it. The bastard raised all the racket to get leverage for negotiations."

Strabo was surprised. "To negotiate what?"

"A place in the *curia*, acceptance into the high society, a larger *domus*, a country villa, his wax mask in the *lararium* once he was gone." There was silence for a while. Verres' comments messed up Strabo's carefully planned interrogation.

"Let me get this straight," Strabo finally said. "Poplicola raised a racket with the masses by promising land distribution to the poor, hoping you and the other decurions would offer him a deal in exchange for his good behavior?"

"At least you got it in one go, sonny. I am impressed." Verres said.

"What about Furius Mus? Was he aware of all this?" Strabo was incredulous.

Veres laughed. "The look on your face." The *secretarius* arrived with a plate of cold cuts, cheese, olives, and a cup of wine. Verres took a swig from the cup to clear his throat, but he didn't offer any to Strabo.

"Furius Mus was the go-between. Mr. High-and-Mighty Poplicola wouldn't dirty his hands." Verres worked himself up. His face reddened as his fat body struggled to keep up with the elevated blood pressure. "Credible deniability, you see. He could always claim he was unaware of Mus' activities if things went south. Thus, every unpleasant detail was handled by Mus while Poplicola continued his noble fight on behalf of the poor masses."

The fucking little mouse! I had underestimated him despite all my vows.

"Let's get back to the beginning. You claim that Poplicola requested to meet over dinner. Was this arranged through Mus?"

"Yes, we had several back-and-forths with Mus during the previous days concerning—how could I put this—Poplicola's cravings. The dinner was supposed to be the final meeting, the one where we agreed on the details and struck a deal." Verres was barely hiding his disgust.

"And I assume this deal involved all the senior magistrates, given the list of participants."

"Mus insisted all of us be present since Merula and Macula would be next year's *duumviri*, and Avitus would enter the final part of his term when he would purge the *curia* and finalize the census. Our friends had trust issues, you see. They wanted guarantees that next year's magistrates would uphold our part of the deal."

Strabo was lost and couldn't quite follow the turn of events. "Could you share more details about the deal?" he said.

"No, you are authorized to investigate Poplicola's death, not to oversee the management of our city. It is enough to say the bastard had a high price but one we were ready to pay." He paused, picked up an olive, looked at it disgustedly, and then tossed it back to the plate. "Thanks for ruining my appetite."

Poplicola was blackmailing the city's elite to get what he wanted, using Mus as a go-between? Something felt off.

"Do you think Poplicola was poisoned because of his demands?" Strabo said.

"As I said, we were willing to pay his price. The alternative—provoking the Emperor and his brother—was even less appealing."

"Are you sure all the other magistrates felt the same as you did? Maybe one of them had second thoughts."

"We had all agreed beforehand," Verres said.

"And still, somebody poisoned Poplicola."

Verres didn't answer, just shrugged in a non-committal way. "I believe we are done here," he eventually said.

"Yes, sir." Strabo rose. "We are done for now. I might need more information about the dinner itself, who sat where, who had access to the kitchen, and so on."

"Feel free to talk to my secretary. He can answer all your questions."

With that, Verres waved Strabo away and signaled his slave to invite the next client in.

******

"Can you take me to the *triclinium*? The one that was used at dinner two evenings ago?" Strabo asked the secretary.

The slave nodded and gestured for Strabo to follow.

They exited into the garden; it was large by Sarmizegetusan standards and stylishly arranged.

Verres had built a second, out-doors dining room in one of the corners. It was the usual setup—three couches arranged around a table—and could accommodate up to nine people.

"Were you in attendance that evening?" Strabo said.

"Yes, sir, I always attend *Duumvir* Verres when he organizes social events at the house."

"Of course you do." Strabo decided to call this one Fussy on account of his body language. "Do you remember the seating arrangements?"

Fussy sniffed and raised an eyebrow, offended by the implication he might not remember the all-important seating arrangements. "*Duumvir* Verres was naturally seated on the main couch, Poplicola to his right as the guest of honor, *Duumvir* Aculeo to his left."

Verres went out of his way to please Poplicola.

By tradition, Poplicola and Mus should have been seated at the other two couches' ends since they had less seniority.

"Who sat on the right couch, the one closest to Poplicola?"

"*Aedile* Macula was closest to Pontius Poplicola. Next to Macula was the other *aedile*, Merula."

"What about the other couch, the one to the left of Verres?"

"Varro, the candidate for next year's *aedile*-ship, sat closest to the host, followed by his partner, Lentulus. Furius Mus occupied the farthermost position."

Strabo stroked his chin, trying to imagine it all. Mus sat diagonally from Poplicola, four other guests between them. Varro and Lentulus were also too far from the victim, with only Verres, Macula, and Merula within arms' reach.

"Tell me, how was the dinner served?" Seeing Fussy's confused grimace, Strabo clarified, "Was the food brought in on individual plates for each of the participants?"

"What kind of house do you think this is?" The secretary was outraged. "All courses were brought in on platters so Master Verres could personally serve his guests of honor. As customary, he attended Poplicola on his right, followed by Aculeo on his left. Finally, the staff attended to the others."

The slaves of the elites are even more snobbish than their masters.

"Same for the wine?"

"Yes, same for the wine. Master Verres mixed the wine with water and served Poplicola first, followed by Aculeo."

Since nobody else got sick, the poison must have been added directly to Poplicola's plate or cup. Verres seemed to be the prime suspect, but Macula was also close enough to do it.

So it was either Verres or Macula. Unless…

"Did anybody leave the table during dinner? To use the facilities, for instance? Or move around the room to engage the other guests?"

"No."

"How can you be so sure?" Strabo said.

Fussy hesitated for a moment before answering in a hushed voice, "It was not a happy affair. Do you know what I mean?" He grimaced. "Everybody was eager to be done with it as soon as possible."

"I see. So nobody left the table, not even for a short while?"

"Wait a minute! Now that I think of it, Furius Mus left the table once." The slave looked into the middle distance, trying to remember the events. "*Quinquennales* Avitus dropped by but refused to join the dinner table. He waited in the *atrium* while I fetched Mus, as demanded by our unexpected guest."

"Then what?" Strabo said.

"Nothing." Fussy shrugged. "I left them in the *atrium*."

"How long were the two of them alone? When did Mus rejoin the table?"

"Let's see. I believe he was out for a quarter of an hour; I had to open the door for Mus after they finished. He walked Avitus out of the house but couldn't re-enter afterward—the door is self-locking."

Why did one of the most influential city fathers request to talk to Mus, not the house's owner? He could have paid his respects, at least.

"Was Avitus on the guest list?"

Fussy sniffed loudly. "He received an invitation but sent his slave a couple of hours before dinner to communicate his unavailability—Avitus was supposedly unwell." Sniff. "When I saw him at the door, I assumed he reconsidered, so

I urged him to follow me to the *triclinium*. But he refused in no uncertain terms—he wanted to talk only to Mus." Fussy recounted. "To think a distinguished man like him would use such unseemly language. It was most inappropriate, I must say!"

"What do you mean?"

"'Bring me that worm, Mus, and be quick about it, you bloody fagot.' That's what he said. Can you imagine?"

He is such a lovely and considerate man, our Quinquennales.

"Appalling," Strabo said. "What happened after Mus rejoined the table?"

"Nothing out of the ordinary; the unhappy gathering lasted for another half an hour. Then, Mus reminded Poplicola of an early appointment the next morning, so they said their goodbyes and left. The other guest followed soon after."

Interesting, Strabo thought. *Verres said they were supposed to agree on a deal.*

"By any chance, have you overheard the dinner conversation?"

"The nerve," Fussy said, folding his arms on his chest. "I would never betray the confidence of my Master."

"But of course not. I wouldn't dream of asking a senior member of the household to betray a confidence," Strabo said. "I was just asking in general terms, you know, for my report. I was expected to use these five silver *denarii* as a reward." He took out the coins from his purse. "But my boss is a hard man, and he wouldn't reimburse my expenses unless I vouched for your full cooperation on this officially sanctioned investigation."

Fussy glanced at the coins pretending no interest. Then, he added, "I guess there is no harm in sharing this with you, *Frumentarie*. No sensitive topic was discussed; it was only polite conversation about the weather, Emperor Severus' successful campaign against the Parthians, and so on."

"You mean they haven't discussed the upcoming elections? Or Poplicola's candidacy?"

"I was within earshot most of the time. If they touched upon local politics, it must have been during my short absence precipitated by Avitus' visit." Fussy shrugged. "But judging by the painfully bored expressions, I doubt anything of interest was discussed."

What the fuck was going on?

Strabo was baffled. Why has Poplicola gathered the city's *crème-de-la-crème*, if not to discuss his demands?

"Thank you for your cooperation," Strabo eventually said, discreetly handing over the coins. "I appreciate your time."

X. A Culinary Puzzle

Strabo arrived at the New Forum. From there, he could cross through the *basilica* and exit in the city's main square, the Old Forum.

He walked at a slow pace, trying to wrap his head around the new pieces of evidence obtained at Verres' house. Nothing made sense anymore.

Let's recap what we have learned.

According to Verres, Poplicola's land distribution platform was nothing but a ploy; his real goal was to blackmail his way to the top. Unless the city fathers gave him what he wanted, he kept rabble-rousing, thus exposing the decurions to massive pressure from the Emperor and his brother, Legate Geta.

Mus was the alleged go-between, acting as a courier between Poplicola and the city fathers.

Poplicola's plan seemed to work; his price was steep, but Verres and company were prepared to pay it. Hence, the dinner requested by Poplicola through Mus—they were supposed to shake hands on the final agreement at the *duumvir*'s house.

Even though it contradicted Mus' claim—that they were running on the land distribution platform out of patriotic duty—Strabo had no reason to doubt Verres' version.

And this is where it gets complicated.

According to Fussy's eyewitness report, all the relevant people attended, but the main topic was not discussed. Not at all. There were no negotiations, no agreements, no oaths, and no signing of documents—just a short and unpleasant dinner filled with meaningless chit-chat.

And then there was Avitus' mysterious visit. Why did he meet with Mus but not the others? What could have prompted the *Head of All the Heads* to come and meet a nobody?

Strabo needed more info—he could talk to Mus again or try Avitus. He wasn't looking forward to either of those interviews, so he parked them for now.

I should focus on the murder itself.

The poison was probably sprinkled directly on Poplicola's plate or cup.

For the sake of argument, the food could have been spiked in the kitchen before it was brought to the table—one of the slaves could have spoiled only a specific part of the platter. In this instance, Verres would have to be involved since he served Poplicola. But this course of action would have been perilous in the extremes. What if the entire platter had been contaminated? Would Verres risk killing the others or even himself? Unlikely.

Poplicola had sat between Verres and Macula, so any of them could have accessed Poplicola's food. Aculeo and Merula could reach the victim's plate or cup, too, but they should have leaned over Verres and Macula, respectively—the others would have surely noticed.

According to Fussy, none left their seats and moved around the table, which ruled out the other guests. And, as the host, Verres served Poplicola—this put the attending slaves into the clear.

Was it Verres, or was it Macula?

It would have been foolish for Verres to poison a guest at his own house with his own hands in front of so many witnesses. Or to encourage someone else to do it. Verres would have been the first suspect, no matter who had poured the poison.

There is a high chance Verres wasn't involved.

Macula, on the other hand, would have more room for maneuvering. He had the opportunity since he was sitting next to Poplicola. Still, since Verres' involvement was unlikely, how could Macula know, in advance, of the seating arrangement?

According to the custom and given his seniority and age, Macula should have been seated to Verres' left. In contrast, Aculeo, as co-*duumvir*, should have been sitting at the place of honor to the right of Verres.

By the same logic, Merula should be seated next since he was the younger *aedile* for this year, followed by one of the candidates.

Varro, Lentulus, Poplicola, and Mus were the same age, the youngest possible age to run for *aedile*-ship—there was no clear seating rule in their case so that Verres could decide the seating on a whim. Consequently, the odds were one-to-four for Poplicola to be seated next to Macula—a rather risky gamble for premeditated murder.

The alternative is that Macula knew Verres would not respect the traditional seating arrangements beforehand. Perhaps he bribed Fussy, the secretary.

There was also the question of the motive; why would Macula poison Poplicola? He was virtually guaranteed to be elected as *duumvir* for the next year together with Merula. Since Poplicola would cease rabblerousing due to the deal they were supposed to seal at dinner, Macula had no apparent reasons to kill him.

Only one way to sort this out; to the forum!

******

People gradually returned to the forum now that lunchtime had passed.

As Strabo entered the *basilica* from the south, he noticed *Duumvir* Acuelo holding court at the eastern tribunal—the current case was a land dispute, by the sound of it.

The *curia*'s meeting hall was empty since the decurions were on break due to the upcoming elections. So was the western tribunal—Verres was not in attendance today.

Strabo spotted his target as soon as he stepped out on the building's other side.

Aedile Macula sat on his *curule* chair, leaning on a foldable desk—he conversed with his co-*aedile,* who set up shop a dozen feet away. Business was slow, with no citizen lined up to talk to either of the two public officials.

"*Salve, Aedile* Macula." Strabo approached them.

"*Salve*, citizen," Macula said. "If you have complaints about the sewage system, please take it up with my colleague.

Today is his turn to take care of the shitty problems." He laughed.

"Very droll, sir. But I have a different kind of shitty problem in mind," Strabo said.

"Is that so?" Macula was a skinny, anxious kind of person. His raven hair was cut short, his dark eyes darting left and right. He had difficulty staying put and tirelessly fidgeted on his chair.

"My name is Lucius Lucretius Strabo, and I am a *frumentarius* attached to the Thirteenth Legion. I am currently investigating the suspicious death of Cominius Pontius Poplicola." Strabo handed over his authorization papers.

"I see," Macula said, handing back the document. "Since Poplicola died on the latrine, maybe this is a sewage problem after all." He laughed again.

"Glad to see you take it in good humor, sir. Your attitude is admirable, that is, for a murder suspect."

"What? Who? Me?" Macula jumped up and down in his chair, blinking in rapid succession. "Suspect? Me? Is this a joke?"

Strabo said, "According to credible eyewitnesses, you were *Duumvir* Verres' guest at the same dinner party at which Pontius Poplicola was poisoned. Were you not?"

"Y-y-yes, I was. So what?"

"You sat next to Poplicola during the dinner, correct?"

Macula bit his fingernails, unable to control his nervousness. He nodded cautiously. "So what?"

"*Duumvir* Verres was within arms reach, too, but he would presumably not poison a guest in his own house, right?"

"Of course. I mean, yes, fully agreed." He paused, then added, "I agree Verres wouldn't poison a guest. Yes, I agree!" He kept nodding.

"Excluding Verres, you are the only one who sat close enough to poison Poplicola's food or drink," Strabo said.

"No." Macula laughed hysterically.

Strabo glanced at Merula, who was listening intently. "Who else?"

"Oh, no, you don't; don't you even think about it," Merula said. "Paetus Aelius was between Poplicola and me. He would have noticed had I done anything suspicious. Wouldn't you, Paetus?"

"Yes, I guess so." Macula was too agitated to sit, so he stood up, pacing between his desk and Merula's.

"*Aedile* Macula, had anybody other than Verres touched Poplicola's plate or cup?"

"No, not that I remember. But why would I kill Poplicola? I liked the man."

Strabo stared at him in silence. *Let him sweat a little.*

"He had guts; I admired that. Poplicola was a nobody, having no wealth or a powerful family behind him, but he still managed to blackmail himself a bright future," Macula said among wild gesticulations.

He thinks I know the content of the mysterious deal, Strabo realized.

"Well, he had a bright future only if the others kept their end of the bargain," Strabo said, baiting Macula.

"It is why Poplicola insisted on the marriage alliance and substantial dowry. Avitus had no choice but to uphold the deal unless he was willing to part with a significant portion of his wealth."

Marriage alliance? What the hell?

Strabo struggled to hide his shock. He said, "Smart move, indeed. What about Aurelia Sexta?"

"What about her? She is still young and quite attractive, and her father has money—she will have no trouble finding a good match." Macula leered. "I might have considered offering myself as a husband, but I guess it is off the table given the circumstances. Do you think she blames all of us for his death?"

"I think you are not doing yourself any favors by adding possible motives for murder next to your name."

Merula chuckled while Macula turned white. "Oh, I didn't mean to do that. I meant...you know what I meant!"

Strabo waved him to silence. "I still don't see how Poplicola obtaining a good deal clears you from suspicion of murder."

"What do I have to gain? I will be elected *duumvir* in a few days, either way. With Poplicola's ambition settled, Merula and I would have had a good year satisfying both the people and the Emperor—a failproof recipe for securing comfortable postings later on. Most likely, we would have received the command of some auxiliaries here in Dacia." Macula shrugged. "It was a win-win deal. The only casualty was Avitus' pride." He laughed.

What kind of deal would have made everybody happy?

Strabo pretended to ponder the issue and then shook his head. "I am still not convinced. You were the only one with the opportunity to poison Poplicola."

Merula finally stood up and walked over to protect his less-gifted friend.

"*Frumentarie*, no one at the dinner table had reasons to kill Poplicola," Merula said. "On the contrary, everybody gained from his scheme—he would have been a valuable addition to the *curia*."

Strabo raised an eyebrow questioningly.

"My agitated friend and I would have had the privilege to distribute half of the land to the Emperor's veterans and the rest to the impoverished citizens of Sarmizegetusa. At the same time, Varro and Lentulus would have secured their election to next year's *aedile*-ship, while Poplicola and Mus would have succeeded them the year after.

Macula butted in, "Even Avitus was secretly relieved because somebody would marry that unfuckable daughter of his."

Strabo couldn't believe his ears. He considered himself a cynic, but this level of opportunistic pragmatism was beyond his powers of comprehension. "No one at the dinner table had reasons to kill Poplicola," he whispered.

"That's right," Merula said. "Everybody was content with the deal."

It stands to reason, then, that the murderer wasn't present.

XI. Love Hurts

Strabo strolled through the vegetable market's stalls, but he wasn't there for shopping—he took a detour to postpone the inevitable. Dark clouds gathered over the city, and the wind swept the dusty streets. He sighed. *No more stalling.*

He walked down the narrow side street and knocked on the now familiar door.

The same skinny slave answered. "Can I help you, sir?" He recognized Strabo, so he continued, "Please come in; Mistress Aurelia is awaiting your arrival."

Strabo followed Skinny to the *tablinum.*

Aurelia Sexta stood next to her late husband's desk. She wore a snow-white *stola* fastened with two belts, one just below her full breasts and the other around her narrow waist. A blood-red *palla* covered her head and shoulders.

She has a beautiful body.

Her sad blue eyes, pale white skin, and raven hair made her look fragile yet stunning.

"I was expecting you, *Frumentarie* Strabo." She smiled weakly and gestured toward the seat in front of the desk. "Please, have a seat. Can I get you something?"

Strabo's throat was dry, and he had to swallow a few times before he could answer. "No, thank you, Aurelia."

"So, how do you want us to proceed?"

"You could tell me what happened," Strabo said.

"Don't be silly." She giggled. "I love stories, especially the sad ones. Would you mind telling me one?" Her pleading blue eyes were irresistible; she had an almost hypnotic effect on Strabo.

"If you promise to help me with the details."

She puckered her sensual lips as if kissing the air and nodded. "I think I can do that."

Strabo cleared his throat again and began in a surprisingly steady voice, "You were deeply in love with Cominius Pontius Poplicola since you were children. You followed and supported him through thick and thin, disregarding the dangers he exposed you to." He paused to allow Aurelia to comment, but she just nodded for him to go on. "Your other childhood friend, Gaius Furius Mus, was at least as much in love with you as you were with Cominius. He worshipped and protected you by repeatedly helping Poplicola get out of trouble".

"Dear Gaius," she whispered.

"After your husband's failed attempts, Mus finally devised a plan which could propel both of them to power. Namely, by promising land distribution to the poor citizens of Sarmizegetusa, they hoped to be elected as *aediles* and into the *curia*. Once in office, they could have gathered enough support to pass the bill—it was only a question of time. Eventually, they would not only attain the highest magistracies in Sarmizegetusa, but their names would be forever etched in the city's memory."

"Gaius was always the smart one." She smiled. "If only I had seen beyond his feeble appearance…."

"But the plan went up in smoke when Legate Geta announced his support for Varro and Lentulus. He made it clear the Emperor planned to distribute the land to his legionary veterans instead of the poor citizens of the *colonia*. Suddenly, your husband's lifelong dream was shattered once again." He sighed, reluctant to go on.

She tilted her head in an interrogative gesture. "Anything wrong?"

Strabo shook his head, sighed again, and continued, "But Poplicola was not about to let this go, was he? He decided to push on with his candidacy, rouse the masses, and then twist the arms of the city fathers until they gave him what he always wanted—a place among the rich and powerful for him and his descendants."

She smiled, her flawless white teeth contrasting with the red sensual lips, but it was a sad smile. Her eyes were full of tears. "Cominius was obsessed with bringing glory to his family. Eventually, his obsession blinded him to our love." She struggled to keep the tears from overwhelming her. "Please, go on."

"So he made a deal with Avitus, Verres, and company. In return for a compromise land distribution bill, Poplicola and Mus would drop out of this year's election and announce their whole-hearted support for Varro and Lentulus. The new bill would ensure that some of the lands would go to legionary veterans while the rest would be distributed to the impoverished citizens of the city. Both the people and the

Emperor would be content with this arrangement, and Poplicola could take partial credit for the legislation."

Her soft laugh sounded as refreshing as a cold mountain river. "It was an elegant way out, you must admit, *Frumentarie* Strabo."

"Yes, but this was only the public part of the deal. Privately, Poplicola requested support to fulfill his personal ambitions. And, whatever he was promised, Poplicola needed guarantees—he doubted the decurions would keep their end of the bargain once the election was over." Strabo gestured apologetically. "I'll need your help, Aurelia. What exactly was promised to Poplicola?"

"Well, I am sure you could figure it out by yourself, but I said I'll help." She beamed the most beautiful smile Strabo had ever seen. "So, I'll be a good girl and humor you."

Strabo felt dizzy; for a fleeting moment, he was worried he might have been poisoned. *But I didn't consume anything.*

Aurelia said, "Cominius and Gaius were promised the gentry's unwavering support for the next *aedile*-ship elections."

"And Avitus' daughter was the guarantee Poplicola was looking for," Strabo added softly.

"That's right. Cominius was supposed to ditch me and marry Avitus' daughter. The *Quinquennales* agreed to provide a substantial dowry of five million with a special clause—if they divorced within three years for any reason, Poplicola would keep the money. In short, he was beholden to her because he needed the gentry's political backing, while she was tied to him because of the dowry money. Furthermore, Avitus has no other children, and no decurion wants to marry the aging and unattractive Hostilia, despite her father's influence. As disagreeable as it might have been for Avitus, Poplicola was probably his only hope for a grandchild."

"No one at the dinner had a reason to kill Poplicola," Strabo said. "But then again, he wasn't murdered there, was he?"

"No, he was not," Aurelia said. She gazed into the middle distance, carried away by her thoughts.

Strabo waited for a while before he nudged her on. "Care to finish the story for me, Aurelia?"

She blinked as if disturbed from deep thought, smiled at him, and nodded.

"I knew about Cominius' scheme since the day he voiced it; Gaius warned me as usual." She shrugged. "At first, I couldn't believe it. I thought Gaius was overreacting, especially since there was no change in Cominius' behavior—nothing hinted at his intention to leave me. Actually, his mood improved as his dream of being accepted into the big league was almost accomplished. He brought me flowers almost daily, and we made love every morning and evening."

She paused to regain her composure and continued, "There were no changes in his political opinions either. After our evening lovemaking, he always talked about how Sarmizegetusa would be born anew due to his land distribution. He raved about how each Roman citizen would turn into so many Cinncinatii and how the Marcomannic invasion couldn't happen again with such extraordinary citizens defending the province."

Aurelia lifted her cup from the desk and took a sip. "Despite all this, my inner voice egged me on. I couldn't imagine my life without him, so I decided to end it if the worst came to pass. Someone told me the autumn crocus was a good option for suicide, so I visited an herbalist and acquired a pouch."

She took another sip. "Then, on the night of the dinner, a slave courier dropped by—Poplicola dispatched an important document for safekeeping." She nodded toward Skinny. "The courier instructed him that under no circumstances was I to see its contents." Aurelia shook her head. "You can't tell a woman she cannot do something and expect her to obey—even without Gaius' warning, I still would have glanced at it. So I did." She grimaced. "Can you guess what it was? An exquisite man like yourself could surely figure it out."

Strabo blushed involuntarily. He was seldom the target of compliments from goddesses in human form. "I assume it was a document signed by Avitus, promising his daughter, dowry and all."

"Smart boy," she said. "It described the whole agreement, bearing Avitus' seal."

She lifted her cup and emptied its contents in one swig. "All my fears were confirmed in black ink on white papyrus. But instead of feeling depressed, my heart filled with rage. After everything I have done for him, Cominius would push me away like a child discards a broken toy. In those moments, all I could think of was revenge."

Strabo sat motionlessly, waiting for her confession.

"When Cominius returned in the evening, he was in an excellent mood, singing to himself. He even tried to make love to me. The nerve! He had just sealed a deal to throw me away but had the gall to use me one last time." Aurelia was red now, her mouth foaming with spittle. Gone was the sensuality that ensnared Strabo. "So I killed him instead of myself. I gave him a large cup of poisoned wine before we went to bed." She shuddered at the memory. "I waited and waited, pretending to sleep. After a while, he began coughing. Then, he vomited on the bedroom floor. When he went to the latrine, I stayed outside the door and listened as he slowly choked to death."

A heavy silence fell on the *tablinum,* and Strabo couldn't decide how to proceed. If he arrested Aurelia, she would be tortured and publicly humiliated before being executed for mariticide.

More than an hour passed as Strabo agonized over his decision. Aurelia sat all this time motionlessly. A coughing fit finally broke her silence. Strabo looked at her in horror, realization dawning on him.

"Oh, no!"

"Indeed, *Frumentarie*, I decided to follow my husband in death." She pointed at the empty cup. "If I meet him beyond the Styx, I might even forgive him." Her laugh was interrupted by another coughing fit. Finally, she reached out and touched Strabo's hand. "Did he ever love me? How could he throw me out without showing any regret?"

Strabo struggled to keep his emotions under control. "Aurelia, do you want me to stay with you until the end?"

"Such a gentleman." A ghost of a smile crossed her face. "I wonder, how could anyone recommend autumn crocus for suicide? It is a shitty way to die, you know." Aurelia chuckled. "Now, please go."

Strabo stood up and walked toward the exit. He turned to see Aurelia's mesmerizing smile for one last time before leaving the house.

"Goodbye, Aurelia," he whispered, tears finally running down his cheeks.

XII. A Friend in Need is a Friend Indeed

The following morning Strabo recounted the whole story to Hilarius, and the Praefect sent a couple of legionaries to retrieve the murderer. They found her soiled corpse leaning over the *tablinum*'s desk.

The news of Aurelia's crime and subsequent death spread like wildfire—the masses were outraged by what they saw as the mindless act of a decadent woman. Always the opportunists, the *curia* immediately passed a bill reinforcing capital punishment for mariticide.

Furthermore, Avitus used his role as *duumvir quinquennales* to clamp down on Roman matrons' immoral behavior. He outlawed revealing clothing, reinstated the ancient law that forbade Roman women to consume wine, and encouraged male citizens to keep a close watch over their womenfolk.

Hilarius was so relieved by the outcome that he was said to have repeatedly smiled during the run-up to the election—Strabo never witnessed the miraculous appearances, though.

Although Varro and Lentulus ran as partners, each citizen had two votes and could cast them however they saw fit. Exploiting the emotions generated by Poplicola's death, Furius Mus was elected *aedile* by the citizens' overwhelming majority. Varro was chosen to be the second *aedile*, while his partner Lentulus' finished a distant third.

Surprisingly to most but not Strabo, as soon as the election results were published, Mus and Varro pledged to submit a compromise land distribution bill—part of the lands would be distributed to the veterans, and the rest would go to the impoverished citizens of Sarmizegetusa.

It is a fucking win-win situation!

******

The memorial service of the late Cominius Pontius Poplicola was held the day after the election. With no close relatives readily available, Mus took it upon himself to organize the lavish affair.

Half of the city gathered to pay their respects near the temple district outside the northern gates, Strabo among them. Poplicola's body was laid on the funeral pyre, with two golden coins covering each eye. The *libitinarii* did a magnificent job—his body was so well preserved despite the passing of the days that one might expect him to stand up and walk away.

As his best friend and organizer of the funeral service, Mus was expected to give the *laudatio funebris*, the customary eulogy—Strabo was only half-listening; he was still depressed by Aurelia's tragic story.

"...and one can only imagine the thoughts of dear Cominius Pontius as he lay paralyzed, waiting for the inevitable death.

Some poisons kill instantly, but the crocus kills slowly and painfully—only an evil woman with darkness in her heart could use it on her loving husband. To add insult to injury, poor Cominius had plenty of time to reflect on a future without him during his long agony. He must have been heartbroken, believing his dream of an equitable land distribution might die with him. But thanks to you, the great citizens of *Colonia* Ulpia Traiana Sarmizegetusa, Cominius Pontius Poplicola's name will be forever remembered as the spiritual father of the bill Varro and I are putting forward in the Assembly. A fair deal that rewards our heroic veterans while it returns many of you to the dignified life of a Roman citizen...."

Strabo couldn't listen anymore without feeling sick. Mus' hypocrisy was nauseating, although Strabo knew from personal experience that the other city leaders were at least as rotten.

He strolled toward the city, hoping to clear his head. He walked for a while, closing in on the gates. Strabo struggled to forget the image conjured by Mus' words—a paralyzed Poplicola, shitting himself to death while contemplating his failure to reach his life-long dream. It was a tragic image— *Hold on a minute!*

How could Mus know about the crocus? Strabo omitted this detail in the final report; '*Death by poison*' is all he had written.

A wave of heat washed over Strabo, and the world turned around him. He fell to his knees, instantly throwing up that morning's breakfast. The realization of his stupidity was overwhelming.

'*Someone told me the autumn crocus was a good option for suicide.*' Strabo recalled Aurelia's words.

"Argh!" Strabo slapped his face. He couldn't believe he had missed something so obvious.

'*I wonder, how could anyone recommend autumn crocus for suicide?*' she had said.

"Nobody in his right mind would recommend *crocus* for suicide!" Strabo shouted to the sky. For suicide, people used fast-working poisons; for assassinations, a slow-working one was more suitable because it allowed the assassin enough time to escape.

Calm down!

Strabo controlled his breathing in an attempt to calm himself—it took him several heartbeats, but he stopped shaking. His vision returned to normal simultaneously with his heart rate.

Strabo tidied up his tunic, wiped the corner of his mouth, and retraced his steps back to the funeral.

The pyre was already alit, the yellow flames licking Poplicola's corpse—Strabo waited patiently for the fire to finish its cleansing work.

Mus watched the smoking ashes, his hands clasped before him, and his head bowed piously.

"My deepest condolences, Furius Mus," Strabo whispered.

"Ah, *Frumentarie* Strabo. Thank you for coming," Mus said, returning to the ashes after briefly glancing at Strabo.

"And congratulations on the election. I am sure Poplicola would have been proud."

Mus smiled. "Yes, I believe he would be." He paused and then said, "I will not let him down."

"Indeed. By the way, that was a powerful eulogy you gave. I especially liked the part where Poplicola recalled his life while being mortally paralyzed."

Mus looked up. "You have morbid tastes, Strabo."

"I wonder, how did you know about the type of poison and the associated symptoms?"

"What do you mean? I heard it from somebody. Surely, the whole city is talking about it," Mus said, trying to deflect.

"I don't think so. We haven't published details about the poison, you see."

"Really? Are you sure, *Frumentarie*?"

Strabo answered through greeted teeth, "Dead sure."

Mus shrugged it off. "Who knows? Maybe it was just a lucky guess."

"Tell me, Mus, did Poplicola really plan to drop out of the race? Has he ever demanded the hand of Avitus' daughter and the exorbitant dowry as a guarantee? And while we are at it, had anyone other than you heard him express his requests?"

There was a long silence between them as Mus kept staring into the ashes.

"I don't know what you are talking about," Mus eventually said.

"Let me spell it out for you. Poplicola never intended to drop out of the race and never instructed you to negotiate with Verres and the others on his behalf. It is why you handled all the communication and the reason why the topic never came up during the dinner—Poplicola had no clue about your dealings."

Mus hadn't reacted, and he kept staring ahead.

"You convinced him to run on the land distribution platform, which you conveniently explained to me. But you realized you could never get the legislation through when Legate

Geta threw his weight behind Varro and Lentulus. Everybody knew you had no chance to derail the Emperor's plans except Poplicola—he was too pigheaded to acknowledge the danger, like so many times before."

Strabo paused again for a couple of heartbeats. "But what looked like a catastrophe could be twisted into a once-in-a-lifetime opportunity if one had the brain and inclination to do so. So you devised the whole scheme—you initiated negotiations with the city's elite on Poplicola's behalf and ensured one of the demands was marriage to Avitus' daughter. Then, you poisoned Aurelia's mind, warning her about Poplicola's alleged plan. How am I doing so far?"

"Admirably, although I have no clue what you are talking about," Mus said without turning away from the smoky ashes.

"You manipulated Aurelia to acquire the autumn crocus and then orchestrated the dinner. I assume you told Verres that

Poplicola didn't want to discuss the distasteful details over dinner. You suggested polite conversation instead—the participation itself was an unspoken acceptance of the mutually beneficial deal. At the same time, you requested a written commitment from Avitus, the guarantor of the whole agreement."

Strabo had to take a deep breath to keep himself calm and steady. "Avitus dropped by Verres' house but refused to stay for dinner, incensed because a nobody twisted his all-mighty arm. Instead, he gave you the stamped document detailing the agreement—Aurelia wasn't convinced by your words alone, especially since Poplicola showed no signs of leaving her, nor had he changed his political stance, so you required written proof."

"I don't know what you are talking about," Mus whispered.

"Verres' secretary told me you left the house presumably to walk Avitus out. But this wasn't true, was it? You had a courier stationed nearby. He delivered the document to Poplicola's house with clear instructions that Aurelia could not see it. You knew very well that, after you planted the seeds of suspicion into her heart, she would jump on any document, especially one that was specifically 'not to be opened by her.'

Mus shook his head wordlessly as Strabo pushed on.

"She saw your warnings confirmed and was furious beyond control. Since you made sure the crocus was on hand, Aurelia used it to poison her husband rather than allowing him to divorce her and marry Avitus' daughter. With Poplicola out of the way, you rode the popular sympathy, won the election, and revived the compromise bill to avoid the Emperor's wrath and secure your longtime career."

Strabo raged by then and could barely keep himself from strangling the *aedile*-elect. "I bet you hoped Aurelia would turn to you now that Poplicola was dead. Tell me, you fucking mouse, did you expect her to marry you?!?" The few remaining attendants turned their heads to see what the commotion was about.

"No, I was not," Mus said dryly. He turned toward Strabo, held his gaze, and said, "I have listened to your story, *Frumentarie* Strabo. Now you listen to mine. I was elected almost unanimously by the citizens of Sarmizegetusa, and because of my political machinations, countless citizens will see an improvement in their sordid lives. Moreover, our city will be safe from invasion, having thousands of legionary veterans settled around it. It is a win-win situation, so to speak. As they say, '*Vox Populi, Vox Dei.*' The voice of the people is the voice of the gods."

"Is Poplicola happy? Or Aurelia?" Strabo said.

"His wife, Aurelia Sexta, murdered Pontius Poplicola. She confessed to none other than you, the official investigator. Do you deny it?"

Strabo bit his tongue. There was nothing clever he could say to that. "What about justice?"

Mus stared at Strabo for a long time, eventually shrugged, and strolled toward the city. He stopped a dozen paces away and turned back to Strabo, a manic grin on his mousy face.

"Justice was served when the man who humiliated me for as long as he lived and the woman who scorned me her entire life killed each other. What more can you expect from goddess Iustitia?"

Strabo watched the back of the departing Mus in silence, Aurelia's words repeatedly ringing in his head.

"Love is all-powerful, Strabo. It can make you do things you'd never thought yourself capable of."

Ave, Lector!

First of all, thank you for purchasing '*Vox Populi: An Agent Strabo Mystery Novella.*'

I know you could have picked any number of books to read, but you chose this book, and for that, I am incredibly grateful.

If you enjoyed it and found some benefit in reading this, I'd like to hear from you and hope you could take some time to post a review on Amazon.

Your feedback and support will help me to improve my writing craft for future projects.

Thank you,

Alex

Books by the Author

The Martyr: A Roma Invicta Story (Book #1)

The "*Roma Invicta*" stories scrutinize the Ancient Roman civilization through the lens of alternate history. Blending historical fiction with sci-fi elements, the novella-length tales reflect the author's well-known style: long enough to be immersive but not to the extent of slowing down the pace.

What if the Roman Empire never fell?

Two thousand seven hundred and seventy-three years after the Founding of Rome, the Empire is stronger than ever. Peace and stability have reigned on Earth for centuries while the invincible legions extend the Pax Romana one star system at a time. However, unseen cracks appear under the façade of invincibility as long-forbidden ideas return to haunt the Empire.

When Marcus Amelius Pius embarks on a transformative journey, the Inquisition sends its best agent to apprehend him. Can Pius awaken the beliefs that once shook the Empire? Or will Inquisitor Ferox prevail?

Step into the alternate universe of "*The Martyr*" to find out!

The Growing Shadow: The City of Kings (Book #1)

Visions of the End Times are haunting the feverish dreams of a dying monk.

Rumors of strange attacks are reported by the patrols of the Northern border.

Trouble is brewing among the great lords of the kingdom as old enemies are requesting refuge against the growing shadow from the East.

Welcome to the City of Kings at the dawn of the First Mongol Invasion of Europe.

Delve into a story of lords and ladies, noble knights and ruthless warriors, mysterious and exotic adversaries, courtly scheming, religious strife, political intrigue, love and grief, and all-out war and senseless bloodshed.

Once you get up to speed with the political intricacies of the day, you'll be rewarded with a fast-paced, action-packed story.